Adva

"Shawna Partri(
fast-paced work
tenderness of a storytelling family. Personal narratives, diary
entries, letters, and historical facts are skillfully
intertwined in this compelling examination of generational
understanding and misunderstanding. Secrets provide the
catalyst for the narrator's probing desire to uncover truths,
reconcile differences, and ultimately determine who, in
light of her family, she is."

- Madeline Sonik, author,
  Afflictions & Departures: Essays

"Shawna Diane Partridge delivers a solid first book –
part love story, part mystery, part self-help…. *Rule of
Seconds* exemplifies what can happen when the tradition of
matriarchal leaders living in patriarchal times get a voice to
speak out. Where 'secrets' aren't so much secrets as they
are purposefully-kept-quiet life choices. Where pride and
face-saving reigned over compassion and hope. Where the
women let their space and time define them on the outside
leaving heaving holes within that could never been filled."

– Vanessa Shields, author of *I Am That Woman*
  and *Look At Her*

"Shawna Diane Partridge is a gifted northern storyteller
who weaves a compelling narrative that is deeply rooted
in place, family, memory, and the immigrant experience.
Rule of Seconds takes us into the lives led by members of
one Ukrainian family that struggled to make ends meet,
both physically and emotionally, throughout the course of
the twentieth century. This is a must read for anyone who
has had a 'hard' maternal immigrant figure in their lives."

- Stacey Zembrzycki, author of *According
  to Baba: A Collaborative Oral History of
  Sudbury's Ukrainian Community*

Rule of Seconds

Rule of Seconds

A Novella

SHAWNA DIANE PARTRIDGE

Publisher's note: This book is a work of fiction. Names,
characters, places and incidents are either the product
of the author's imagination or are used fictitiously, and
any resemblance to actual persons living or dead is
entirely coincidental.

Library and Archives Canada Cataloguing in Publication
Partridge, Shawna Diane
Rule of seconds / Shawna Diane Partridge
ISBN: 978-0-9949183-2-1 (paperback)

I. Title

PS8631.A79R85 2016   C813'.6   C2016-902108-4

Printed and bound in Canada on 100% recycled paper.
Book & Cover Design: Carousel Photography & Design
Author's Photo: Ashley Elizabeth Gordon, AEG Designs

Published by:
Latitude 46 Publishing
info@latitude46publishing.com
Latitude46publishing.com

To 'hard' women.

The way the past unfolded depended upon who told it.

Or So It Was Said

It begins, always, with the eyes. The day began with thunder, then heavy rain punctuated by lightning strikes so near the house they rattled the windows. That morning, I had a strange feeling. My doctor calls it the aura, a warning of a seizure. The timing, always unpredictable. Doesn't matter what doc calls it. When it hits, eyes twitching, legs and arms spasming, lips mumbling, incoherent, speech, inconceivable, mouth frothing, jaw out of control, grinding the tongue, taste of blood. Inside, shouting, *God, make it stop. Speak! Why can't I speak? Yell! Yell for help! God, oh please, let me black out.* It begins with the eyes. Uncontrolled blinking. Strobe lights. That aura. Cruel warning. Something. I can't prevent. Coming.

Today the diviner arrived. Herald Hudy, water witch and a messenger transcending the future, would reach down, penetrate the earth's secrets, locate springs hidden deep underground, say, where to dig the well. Herald was a close family friend on my mother's side. Herald stood on deathly thin legs, wore pants that were too short but too large for his skeletal waist, crowned his head with a feathered hat, had partial-to-no teeth, and on his bicycle mapped the city of Sault Ste. Marie.

My mother Izza was thirteen when Herald envisioned her future. He foresaw that Izza would give birth to two girls, but before then she would choose between two men prior to marrying one of them.

So the prediction goes: "Izza, you will attract two suitors who live in opposite ends of the city."

Growing up, Izza lived in the Buckley area in Sault Ste. Marie, Ontario near the industrial park in the city's West End. Beginning at a young age, Izza had grown accustomed to the grey smog and noxious clouds billowing from the Steel Plant's stacks in the near distance. She tried to ignore the stench. In a three-room bungalow, she spent her childhood. That bungalow had seven unused windows. During times when the Steel Plant ramped up production, those seven windows were not to be opened. Izza's mother detested the stench of sulfur that emitted from the Plant. Reeking of rotten eggs, the sulfur curled out of the stacks and crept its way into that Buckley bungalow through the outside dryer vent, warped frame of the front door, all sorts of cracks. The invisible pong permeated the house, latched onto fibres, diverted thoughts.

Like other houses in Buckley, the bungalow was sheathed in sheets of imitation brick siding. In that fake-brick bungalow, a happy traditional family could have lived. Instead, a gang of sundry persons inhabited the house and its three bedrooms. In one bedroom, my grandparents No-No and Ollie relaxed away from their children at night. Ollie outfitted the two other bedrooms with hand-carved bunk beds. Three of No-No and Ollie's four children, including Izza, occupied the second bedroom. Izza was the second oldest of the four children. For her elder sibling status, she received the bottom bunk and left her younger brother and sister to squabble over the top bunk and the lack of adequate space it provided. In the third and final bedroom, the eldest sibling in the family, along with four to five Aboriginal student boarders, piled themselves one on top of the other. The third bedroom managed only to fit two bunk beds within its close walls. No-No refused to furnish or decorate the room beyond the two far-from-gently-used bunk beds. Those student boarders stayed only for the school year. Each year would only usher in a new cohort of boisterous boarders to that Buckley bungalow and with it bring the same assignment of bedrooms.

In the 60s and 70s, the Buckley neighbourhood was lined with young families. Izza and her three brothers and sisters had plenty of children their own age to befriend if they wished. In a fenced yard, they chose to play by themselves. Izza and her older brother Allen knew the neighbourhood gossip. They tried to stay in their own backyard and out of earshot to hear conversations between the neighbourhood busybodies. Izza and Allen hoped their younger brother and sister didn't know what others said about their family. Their efforts would fail. Through the backyard fence their younger siblings would hear the gossip, but they'd be too young to understand grown-up conversation. They'd ask for explanations. Izza and Allen would refuse.

When I was thirteen, Mother confessed her embarrassment about the family's living arrangements. "I was ashamed of how our family appeared to our neighbours. They'd snicker, 'A blended household.' But why did that matter? Gossips exaggerate, and fib. Our family was always the target of gossip. But never you mind it." She accompanied her lesson with a long explanation. "If you're going to hear stories about the family, you might as well hear them from me. I know what it was *really* like living in that bungalow and neighbourhood. Growing up, the neighbours thought our family was poor. It wasn't like we were as well-off. We managed. We were like everyone else. In the neighbourhood, most households had three to six children, a stay-at-home mother, and a father who worked at the Steel Plant. In those days, it seemed like all the men in the city worked at the Plant. It employed something like ten-thousand workers, not like nowadays. That number has dropped significantly. Back then, our family did okay though, survived. Some people thought, well, maybe your grandma No-No took in boarders because your grandpa Ollie didn't earn enough money at the Plant. Some people thought your grandpa was always too sick to work. Maybe he was like his dad, Andriy, drinking away his paycheques. Some people had no way of knowing how much your grandpa earned. But some people figured they knew everything, knew what was going on in our bungalow. They didn't. They couldn't. All those neighbours could do was gossip. And they did."

No-No was my great-grandmother Anichka's daughter. No-No had learned from her mother to save for those rainy days when something extra would be needed, like when Steel Plant workers were on strike. During those times, my grandfather had no paycheque while he and other labourers waited for union representatives to negotiate with company men for improved wages and benefits.

Another of Mother's lessons that I had to remember: "Strikes don't have expiration dates you see? Strikes could last for weeks or even months. No-No had to prepare for unforeseen events. She had to take in boarders. She had to put aside a little somethin' just in case of emergency. You see?"

Every day, gossip circulated through the Buckley neighbourhood. New parts of stories surfaced or juicier rumours took precedence over yesterday's news. Every day, engines roared in the early morning when the men left for work at the Steel Plant with their aluminum lunch boxes in hand. Every day, women waved at each other across the street but when backs were turned, whispered through lipstick-stained teeth. Every day, children played Kick-The-Can in narrow backyards. And Izza habitually watched and listened. She knew what was said not only about her family, but about the other neighbours too. She abhorred what they called "harmless hearsay." Consumed by curiosity, Izza had to know the latest neighbourhood gossip.

Izza was in her late teens when rumours surfaced about her prospect of marriage or lack thereof. Aging busybodies became transfixed on learning about the lives of the street's younger generation. For that reason, heads turned and eyes gawked at adolescent Izza. The busybodies predicted she would become an old maid. In that imitation brick bungalow, Izza would stay forever as No-No's companion. She would be labelled "a spinster." Her name, Izza, would forever be attached to that word "spinster."

But. There was Ronnie. He was a friend of Izza's older brother Allen. Whenever he visited the house, Ronnie smiled at Izza. Sometimes Ronnie waved from the street as he walked by and said, "Hi Izza." Since high school, Ronnie sent little love notes to her. He praised her brown eyes, her high cheekbones, her slender body. With each note, Izza shredded the letter along with Ronnie's unwelcome words. She disposed of the letter and his affection. Izza feared others might learn of Ronnie's fondness for her. Gossip might travel through the neighbourhood, household-to-household, door-to-door, ear-to-ear. Izza especially didn't want Allen to discover Ronnie's affection or desire. Ronnie and Allen ran with the grown-up crowd, three years older than Izza. Allen didn't allow Izza to join his group. She was too young and not cool. She was his little sister. If he happened to learn about Ronnie's affection for Izza, Allen would feel obligated to protect his family. Izza was his sister after all. More than anything, Izza dreaded the embarrassing taunts from her older brother. Allen wouldn't allow his friends to date Izza, but that didn't mean he couldn't poke fun at his little sister for it.

Izza's fears were realized. One day, Allen overheard two neighbours blathering. The gossips mused, "Perhaps she'll marry Ronnie." His visits to see Allen became more frequent as Izza matured. On Ronnie's next visit to see his friend, and Izza, Allen blindsided Ronnie with a punch, resulting in a black eye for the lover-boy. Izza heard shouting, "That's for my sister, you stay away from her. Ronnie, I mean, dude, what were you thinking? Crushing on my sister. Gross. You better leave before I really get mad. And don't bother talking to me at school and don't you fuckin' dare speak to my sister in or outside of school. Jeez, Ronnie, man, you're such an idiot. My little sister? Really?" Escorting a bruised eye and ego, Ronnie slinked down the street and out of the neighbourhood.

In the weeks that followed the one punch fist-fight, Allen and Ronnie would repair their friendship. Ronnie would promise he had no more romantic feelings for Izza, that he had come to his senses.

Years forward, Izza was lean, twenty. After seven o'clock, she refused to eat, wanted to stay thin to appear appealing. She applied lipstick, highlighted her cheekbones, styled her hair for those nights at the local bars.

Izza and her friend Cathy socialized at The Vic in the city's downtown. Cathy started dating Greg. Izza used to call him "Grubby Nails Greg" because of his grimy hands. Cathy never found out about Izza's nickname for Greg. Two words, "Grubby Nails," might have ended their friendship. If they had, Cathy may have never introduced Izza to one of Grubby Nails' friends, Jon.

Mother recounted the story to me one day, "Cathy thought I should see Jon. And Cathy, she was already dating Grubby Nails Greg. Cathy and Grubby Nails, me and Jon could be a foursome. But I wasn't going to be forced into anything, especially with anyone associated with Ole Grubby Nails. You do the same. Stick to your guns."

Jon and Greg both worked at the Steel Plant as general labourers. They'd started straight out of high school. Jon had thick curly hair. And clean blue eyes. He was nothing like his friend Greg. Jon lived with his parents and younger brother in the city's East End, close to Queen Street East. The East End wasn't developed much yet. Its suburbs were small and surrounded by bush. Just like other houses in the East End, Jon's childhood home was built in the early 1960s. Most were bungalows with sharp white siding. But Jon's home was made of brick. Uncultivated bush sheltered the backyard of that brick home. Its backyard seemed to go on for miles, running into wilderness. Jon and his brother escaped from their parents into that bush, built forts and pretended to be pioneers discovering new lands until their mother stood on the back step calling them to dinner. His childhood, his home, were exotic.

Even at twenty, Izza had never ventured to the city's East End. The West End had everything she needed, like shops and markets. She had never travelled further east in the city than The Vic, downtown. Until she met Jon.

When they walked out together, Izza and Jon strolled on the boardwalk alongside St. Mary's River toward the rapids. Jon talked about his life. Izza desired to know all about his neighbourhood, his home, his childhood. She compared her life to his. His small neighbourhood. His sheltered home. His family. His parents and one sibling living alone in a bungalow didn't match her own experience. Jon nicknamed Izza, "My West End Girl." She was proud of the title because of who gave it to her, not for what it represented. She asked Jon not to use her nickname in public. Walking beside Jon, Izza hoped strangers would think she was his East End Girl. If only she didn't have tan skin, dark brown hair and eyes like her Ukrainian parents. Izza longed for blue eyes, like Jon.

Gossip flowed through Izza's neighbourhood. Izza was dating a boy from the East End. At the same time, Ronnie's visits to see Allen, and Izza, became more regular. Secretly, Ronnie presented her with more love letters. The garbage became increasingly full with torn paper.

No-No discovered the letters, pieced them together, and read Ronnie's loving words to Izza. No-No lectured her daughter, "Yes Ronnie's a bit silly, but he'll always live in the West End, close to your family. Marry this other boy, and yous'll end up living in the East End. Is that what you want? To live so far from your family? I'm telling you this right now, I'll never visit yous in the East End. Let me tell you, I'd have to pack a lunch just for the drive to the other side of town. I'd die from starvation along the way. No, the East End's too far from your home. Listen Izza, read Ronnie's letters. He won't put up with this for much longer. Enough with this other boy. Hear me? Ronnie, and that's final."

Four years after they met at The Vic, Izza and Jon eloped. Only their mutual friends, Cathy and Grubby Nails Greg, attended the ceremony to act as witnesses to the marriage. Later that night, Izza and Jon revealed the news to each of their parents. Jon would become my father.

After the elopement, Ronnie's letters and visits all but disappeared.

My parents Izza and Jon bought a brick bungalow in the East End. Housed in real brick, the bungalow was two blocks from my paternal grandparents' home and one block from the main thoroughfare, Queen Street. That bungalow had three large bedrooms. In later years, my parents would furnish each room with a queen-size bed, accent pieces, finely mounted photographs and paintings of the St. Mary's River.

Even in the worst weather, Mother would open the windows to let in the odourless air. The stench of rotten eggs from the Steel Plant stacks didn't carry as far as our home in the East End.

Herald Hudy, diviner, water witch, messenger,

hadn't foreseen all. He hadn't seen the future and continual strife that thirteen-year-old Izza would eventually have with No-No over the location of my parents' bungalow, my childhood home. Herald had read Izza's palm and thought he understood her placid disposition, her father's temperament. Mother did seem placid when there was no other choice. Not when it came to my father, Jon. Herald had been wrong. Mother took after No-No. She took after her own mother. Anichka and the women who followed her were all impulsive, and hard.

Chops or Steaks

It wasn't the first time that women on my mother's side had acted on impulse.

Years later, family members would remember how that particular summer day had turned so suddenly. It was 1923. A warm air current rose above the earth's surface. Lightning webbed across the sky and etched the city's profile. The storm struck quickly. They'd say it was a sign. Bad luck would rain.

Polina and Alexander Fedorenko living in Ukraine had four children, two boys and two girls. Anichka was the second eldest. Anichka, stocky, brazen, and with a strong will, was considered plain by her family and community. Her skin was rough, her fingers, short and thick. Every month, she held in those hands a letter written from her aunt Olla.

Years before, Aunt Olla and Uncle Bohdan had migrated from Ukraine to Canada seeking new opportunities. In her letters, Olla enclosed tokens from Canada: postcards, maps, photographs, even news-clippings. Sometimes those Canadian tokens featured text written in the English language. Growing up in Ukraine, Anichka learned to read and write Ukrainian. She could only guess at the meanings of the English words printed on Olla's tokens.

As the expressive storytellers in my family often told it: Anichka would run her fingers over the embossed letters. The lettering and grainy paper would feel smooth against her rough hands.

Generations later, I discovered an aged postcard in No-No's cluttered house. On it, a name was handwritten in Ukrainian:

Анічка

As a fourth-generation woman of Ukrainian descent, I couldn't read or write in my ancestor's native language. Generations ago, those skills and other cultural traditions faded out. At home and throughout my schooling, I learned to speak, write, and read in English. I could only recognize the Ukrainian spelling of my great-grandmother's name.

I assumed the handwriting on that aged postcard to be that of my great-great-great aunt Olla's calligraphy. Below her rounded lettering: a portrayal of whooshing water with fluid painter strokes accenting each wave and carving out the white caps in the river.

The caption in English:

Hundreds of years ago, this area was called Baawitigong, "Place of the Rapids" by Aboriginals. During whitefish season, the banks of the St. Mary's River was the meeting place of the Ojibwa people.

I placed the postcard in my purse, escaped from No-No's house without being seen, and once at home hid the postcard in the pages of my diary. I protected it from prying eyes, like my mother's judgement.

It would be passed down through the generations how Olla and Bohdan had acquired bits of the English language after years of living in Canada. They had found fellow Ukrainians to befriend and bargain with, so Ukrainian had remained as their primary language, spoken and written. Acquisition of the English language wasn't a necessity for them and their lives.

Olla wrote in Ukrainian when corresponding with her niece. Olla told of her new home in Sault Ste. Marie, Ontario. She described the violent rapids, the river serving as the dividing body, the border, between Canada and the United States. Struck by how exotic Sault Ste. Marie seemed, Anichka would act on impulse and immigrate to the Place of the Rapids. Olla and Bohdan would sponsor her; they would have already been permanent residents of Canada. At first, Anichka would live with them.

1922. While waiting on the wharf, Anichka gripped the ticket in her hand. She travelled alone, first to Halifax, and then continued on to Sault Ste. Marie.

She possessed few personal effects, only a suitcase containing some articles of clothing, along with all the letters and tokens that Olla had mailed her.

Anichka's immediate family stayed in Ukraine. Polina contracted pneumonia shortly after her daughter's immigration. The family insisted the frigid temperatures in Ukraine that year had killed Polina, mother of four. It was foretold since childhood that frail Polina was destined to die too young. The prediction had come true. None of Polina's relations were surprised by her passing.

Much beloved, Polina had a regal burial attended by all who were close to her, except Anichka, Olla and Bohdan. Working-class citizens, they couldn't afford the voyage home to Ukraine. After the funeral, Anichka's father would write, colourfully depicting his wife's grand and final departure.

A friend in Sault Ste. Marie, Nicholas Vovk, visited often to console Anichka after the passing of her mother. Nicholas was a fellow immigrant from Ukraine. Speaking in their native tongue, they shared stories about their childhoods and families, disclosed loneliness over their distant homeland.

Family storytellers would later remark that Nicholas had unruly curly hair. It was the same shade as his thoughtful eyes.

Shortly after meeting Nicholas, Anichka attracted the attention of Walter Miko. Walter worked at a small butcher's shop in the city's West End. Walter always had food and sometimes would bring chops or steaks when he visited Anichka at her aunt and uncle's house. Anichka calculated that Walter Miko would be a reliable man, a well-heeled husband with a steady job who could put food on the table. Although she welcomed visits from the ever attentive Nicholas, a few months into her residency in Canada, Anichka became engaged to Walter Miko. She desired to form family ties, here, in Sault Ste. Marie, in Canada. Perhaps Nicholas could attend the ceremony as her friend. Perhaps he could even witness her marriage to Walter Miko.

Little description of Anichka's fiancé would be passed down through generations of the family. Walter Miko's appearance wouldn't be remembered. Family members would remember the chops and steaks that he had flowered Anichka with. Relations would remember how two weeks before the wedding, Walter gave a store-bought wedding dress to his future bride. Anichka hung the garment in her closet. It waited for their day of union.

Years later, Anichka would boast to her daughters about how that wedding dress was brand new and not second-hand. It was mid-calf length, typical of the popular style at the time. She would crow about that wedding dress made of an eggshell white satin with long sleeves and a fine lace hem.

Gossip also survived about when Anichka actually wore her wedding dress and the circumstances surrounding the day.

July 9, 1923. Sometime before the actual wedding day, Anichka donned that eggshell white dress with the long sleeves and lace hem. Its train flowed after her as she dashed from her aunt and uncle's house toward the Paroisse Sacre Coeur. It was there, at that church, that Nicholas awaited her arrival. It was on that day that a warm current of air rose above the earth's surface. Lightning began to web across the sky, etching the city's profile. The storm struck quickly. Heavy rain followed. And with it, bad luck. And scandal.

Series Circuit

On a similar day, I lay in my bed. The night had been warm but soon rain began cooling the city. Lights filtered through the blinds and caused bars to flicker across my bedpost with every snap of thunder. I ignored the flashing, and slept.

The thunder cracked. I awoke. Eyes flickering. Hyperactivity in my brain, rapidly disseminating, from one cluster of cells to the next and onward. A grid of energy swept across my brain until all the nerve cells fired at once, rippling through my body and short-circuiting my system. The electrical storm, outside, echoed the explosions igniting throughout my body. My body twisted, twitched, spasmed. Thunder cracked, wind snarled, rain plummeted to the ground like hard lies.

Eventually the night sky calmed, and so did my brain and body. Days later, I'd dream of thunder-clouds pulsing in the sky, bolts waiting to strike. My seizures typically struck after I'd fallen asleep, rarely when I was awake and could sense the aura of something coming.

I was thirteen when my first seizure struck. When I was older and focused more on my health, I began researching the malady, studying medical texts and encyclopaedias. I also discovered Mother's diary. In it, I read her account of my first seizure.

2001, Sheila's first seizure. 13 years old. I heard noises coming from her bedroom. Went to check on her. Didn't realize it at the time but she was having a grand mal attack. Her eyes flickering. She couldn't move or speak. She was foaming at the corners of her mouth and wet the bed. It lasted several minutes, maybe seconds. Afterwards she seemed dopey and sick to her stomach and had difficulties walking and speaking. She had some trouble remembering what had happened. Partial memory loss. The seizure happened just after midnight. Jon called the ambulance. We had to be sure she was going to be alright. The paramedics tried to get her to talk. She wasn't making much sense. She was hospitalized for 3 days. The nurses watched over her. The doctor ran some tests. Day before the seizure Jon had primed her bedroom walls. We just wanted to cover the dark red paint and colour her room a nice purple. Could the strong paint smell have caused the reaction? I hope not. If only, I was strong like Anichka was with her own family.

Nicholas Vovk stood outside the Paroisse Sacre Coeur in his chalky work boots and light grey suit he'd borrowed from a friend. Nicholas couldn't fit in his friend's fancier shoes and there wasn't enough time to borrow from anybody else. Nicholas was waiting on his next paycheque so he couldn't buy finer or newer attire, or footwear. Anichka didn't take mind of Nicholas' dress as she dashed toward the church. She grabbed his hand and opened the church doors. Nicholas complimented Anichka on her wedding dress. Anichka complimented Nicholas on his combed hair; she'd never seen him so well-groomed before. The priest waited, Bible in hand, as Anichka and Nicholas walked down the aisle.

So it's been rumoured.

Meanwhile at his family home, Walter Miko rocked on the front porch and added another layer of polish to his evening shoes. Those shiny shoes were almost ready for his and Anichka's wedding day.

Anichka and Nicholas faced priest. Nicholas concealed a modest ring that his mother had lent him in his jacket pocket. After the rushed nuptials, he would have to return the wedding ring to his mother and buy one for his bride, his wife Anichka.

Walter Miko returned his glimmering dress shoes to their appropriate place in his closet. He took out his suit jacket and began brushing its shoulders and upper back. Since the engagement, he'd performed that ritual every Sunday evening. Since childhood, his closet had always contained two fitted suits for church on Sundays.

Anichka leaned in to kiss Nicholas. The priest had pronounced them to be wife and husband.

Walter Miko, his mother and father assembled around the dinner table. The dining chair beside Walter was empty. He and his family delayed serving dinner for Anichka's arrival. They were having steak.

The meat became cold. The fat started to congeal. Walter Miko returned to the front porch to watch for passersby. His parents ate their dinner, no waste.

Anichka wed Nicholas Vovk. She wore the wedding dress paid for by the well-intentioned Walter Miko. Whatever happened to Walter? The Vovk family would never know. Did he ever get the opportunity to wear his dazzling dress shoes and perfectly tailored suit? Did he stay in Sault Ste. Marie? Did he ever confront Nicholas for stealing his bride? Did Walter ever come across Anichka again? Little's known.

Anichka and Nicholas Vovk would have eight children together. They'd live in a neighbourhood in the West End, close to the St. Mary's River. Throughout their youth, their children would swim in the dangerous rapids. Brave but rash, the fifth eldest child would become my grandmother No-No.

These many years later, I've landed a position as the Archivist at the Centennial Library in Sault Ste. Marie. Ninety-one years have passed since the priest forged the bond between my great-grandparents.

Last week, searching through genealogical archives, I discovered their marriage records. Anichka and Nicholas, their names preserved, written in smooth cursive embellished with swoops and flicks of the pen. I assumed the writing to be the priest's hand as neither Anichka nor Nicholas could write in English at that time. When touching the pages, running my fingers along my great-grandparents' names, I imagined Anichka rushing to the Paroisse Sacre Coeur in the wedding dress paid for by another man.

A Three-Storey View

I visited Mother for no other reason than to say hello. That day, she was alone. Father was working the dayshift at the Steel Plant. He wouldn't be home until after five o'clock that evening. Upon entering the house, I realized she had gone out. I took the opportunity to read more of Mother's diary to learn about our family history. By then, everyone in my family had become aware of my epilepsy. I wondered if Mother had ever noted that disorder in any other relation. I skimmed the pages of her diary, glancing at the headings:

Anichka
Love triangles
Men at the Steel Plant
"Broken neck" accident
Alfred in his suit

Since my childhood, Mother passed on stories about my great-grandparents. This is what I can remember of those histories, like the family lore about the three-storey boarding house.

Anichka and Nicholas, heads of the Vovk family, owned a boarding house on Queen Street West, close to the boundary between the West and East End of Sault Ste. Marie. Enclosed within its block, Queen Street West housed a community of Ukrainian immigrants including Aunt Olla and Uncle Bohdan who lived only two streets from the boarding house. Though Anichka was too stubborn to admit it, she relished the familiarity of being surrounded by her people. The Ukrainian language she spoke with neighbours flowed, streaming with memories of her homeland.

The Vovk family included Anichka and Nicholas' eight children, from eldest to youngest: Wasyl, Alfred, Juanita, Oskar, No-No, Audrey, Ruby, and finally Brucie. All eight children had solid frames like Anichka. As the children grew, the more they took after her. A devoted mother, Anichka was stouthearted and shrewd.

In many ways, Anichka was a single mother most of the time. Nicholas was either working at the Steel Plant or catching up on sleep after nightshift, or resting before the graveyard post. He had little time to spend with the children or his wife after working twelve-hour days. Such was the life of a shift worker.

Anichka ran the boarding house. She managed bookings for the rooms and looked after the boarders' needs. Though busy, she was a constant figure around the house. Any of the children needed only to shout "Mom!" and the call echoed through the different levels until it reached her ears. She responded immediately, often chastising her children for shouting.

That three-storey boarding house was the children's playground once their chores were finished and when Anichka wasn't watching. She detested unnecessary noise and commotion. There was too much work, too many floors, and too many people coming and going for her eight children to be running wild.

The children nicknamed their home "The Palace." The Palace didn't have marble floors, lavish drapes, rugs, or ornate furniture, nor did it display priceless paintings or artifacts along the staircase, or the hallways, or in the rooms. The bulk of the rooms featured wooden panelling painted white, drafty windows, and cold hardwood floors. The top floors were hot in the summer. And such a large house was expensive to heat properly in the winter. Nevertheless, the children saw their playground as a palace. The multiple floors and rooms provided ample hiding places during games of hide-and-seek. Each doorway concealed a secret land the children could explore. Anichka referred to the boarding house as "A Place of Work." That was her nickname for it.

Algoma Central Railway workers, ACR for short, were the main occupants of the eight bedrooms on the third floor. The workers needed a place to sleep between shifts or somewhere to rest during their days off. Their families and homes were far away during times when they worked on the rail. Anichka preferred renting to fellow Ukrainians, but money was all the same colour to her. Each boarder's room had a white metal bed in the centre, a bedside table, a closet, a sink, and yellowy floral curtains covering a small window.

The children never played on the third floor. It was the quiet zone during all hours of the day and night. There was always at least one boarder sleeping. The only exception allowed was when one of the children was sent to clean the boarders' rooms. Otherwise the eight brothers and sisters had to remain on the first and second levels.

The children listened to their mother when she issued the no trespassing rule about the third floor. Anichka was not to be disobeyed. Besides, the shifty and hairy and dirty men inhabiting the top floor weren't to be trusted. The children feared what those men might do to them if the shift workers ever stopped yawning and ranting about having to go back to the railyard, to work.

Anichka and Nicholas and their eight children populated the second floor. It housed a small kitchen, dining area, modest living room, along with one larger bedroom and two smaller rooms for all eight children. Each of the children's rooms had two bunk beds. Beds and bickering crowded the rooms. A threadlike partition separated the boys from the girls. The larger bedroom could have hardly been called "the master suite." It contained a large bed, dresser, and closet. When they weren't completing their chores, the children played board games in the living room. Anichka loved board games because they entertained the children for hours and kept them quiet. Monopoly and Snakes and Ladders were the children's favourites.

On the first floor in the long front room, Anichka operated a pool hall. Billiards was a game for the grownups. The eight brothers and sisters weren't allowed near the billiard tables. They were too young to play pool. Rules were Anichka's way of being motherly, because it wasn't in her nature to be affectionate. She equipped the front room with two eight foot tables with slate beds, made in the late 1930s. The fee to play was five cents. Two rounds of pool equalled the cost of a ticket to the movie theatre. Anichka was reasonable when it came to matters of money, on occasion.

Those are all things I've been told, things I remember. But the past can disappear the way the boarding house eventually did. The space formerly occupied by the three-storey home has been taken over by a massive concrete pillar for the International Bridge between Sault Ste. Marie, Ontario and Sault Ste. Marie, Michigan. The bridge connects the Twin Saults.

Recently during the summer, Mother took me to see the lot that the boarding house had stood on. I'd never seen the site before. She pulled the sedan over to the curb and stopped on Queen Street West. The bridge towered above us and concealed the afternoon sun. We stood hidden in the bridge's shadow.

"The boarding house stood over there, where that pillar is. Instead of a pillar, imagine a tall, thin three-storey boarding house. Can you picture it?"

Mother's face turned toward the pillar. It occurred to me that she had inherited Grandmother's sloped nose, a trait No-No shared with her three sisters.

Throughout their lives, Great-Grandmother Anichka and the women who followed her were solid, erect, and immovable.

1968. Some family members praised Anichka for purchasing nine burial plots in a row. She was thinking of the family. She was thinking of her children. It was three years before Nicholas passed away. Anichka noticed her husband's changing complexion and wanted to be prepared. She purchased plots for herself and Nicholas, and one for each of her seven living children.

1971. Nicholas died of a heart attack at the age of seventy-three. Anichka lived sixteen more years. Within that time, she suffered three strokes. During the one that was to be fatal, she stood alone in the basement of her home. She climbed the stairs to the kitchen to dial for emergency. Anichka was eighty-three.

It was sunny the day my great-grandmother Anichka died. Newspapers in the archives show that Sault Ste. Marie experienced a high of seventy-three degrees Fahrenheit that day.

On the thirteenth anniversary of Anichka's death, Mother described the funeral to me. I wasn't in attendance. Anichka passed away two months before my birth. Mother depicted the commotion, "Family and friends gathered at the funeral home to honour

27

your great-grandma. The room containing the casket brimmed with voices. Laughter overshadowed any expression of mourning. You see? No one cried. Wasyl, the eldest child in the Vovk family, was named the executor of your great-grandma's estate. In the will, Wasyl was given the power to assign burial plots to his brothers and sisters as he saw fit and depending on the order they died."

2011. Wasyl passed away at the age of seventy -three in his home in Sault Ste. Marie. He died before his other brothers and sisters. Some family members said Wasyl died of lung cancer. Some said it was a heart attack like Nicholas. Others thought it might've been a stroke because meeting such an end was common in our family, apparently. No-No proposed a different view, that her brother Wasyl died of stage fright. She thought Wasyl was too timid to be the executor to Anichka's estate. Before his death, Wasyl hadn't given a single burial plot to any of his brothers or sisters, not even to himself. As a result, he wasn't buried beside his parents. After his passing, Wasyl's wife bought two plots, one for each of them. Most of the good locations for burial sites were already taken, like plots on a small hill overlooking the cemetery. Each year since 1968, the price of plots escalated. Wasyl's and his wife's plots were expensive and near a dirt road that ran through a large memorial park. The busy road was the hearse route through the park. No-No said that Wasyl and eventually his wife didn't get a whole lot of rest at their resting places.

Then. Great-Aunt Juanita became the executor

because she was the next oldest after Wasyl. No-No suspected Juanita had given a burial plot to each of their two younger siblings. Ruby and Brucie had been granted a plot each, although No-No was not. Grandmother had no way of knowing exactly what Juanita had done. They hadn't talked in years. Juanita couldn't cope with No-No's temper. And No-No was angry at most of her siblings and the majority, if not all, of the relatives on my grandfather's side of the family. She complained about not receiving a burial plot or at least word about what happened to the sites. And she complained that Juanita inherited more of Anichka's money than the rest of the siblings. Once, Juanita tried to reason with No-No. Juanita explained how all their brothers and sisters were present at the reading of the will. They all heard how the money was to be divided evenly among the siblings. No-No refused to accept the explanation, largely because it came from Juanita. Those two had never agreed on anything.

Everyone knew that Great-Grandmother had accumulated her wealth by operating a drinking establishment. She'd also earned thousands when the City of Sault Ste. Marie bought the boarding house and most of the homes on Queen Street West. Like many homes in the neighbourhood, the boarding house was demolished in the early 1960s so that construction on the International Bridge could begin.

1988. Year of my birth. Great-Grandmother Anichka passed away with savings of half a million dollars.

It was No-No's eighty-second birthday. I visited

her at my grandparents' house in the West End. They lived a few blocks from where the boarding house once stood.

About twice a month, I visit my grandparents and travel from my apartment building in the East End to the West End of town, past the site of the pillar. The massive concrete pillar causes me to recall stories about that drafty three-storey boarding house, about Anichka and her daughters.

It was gusty that day No-No turned eighty-two. The air carried the reek of rotten eggs from the Steel Plant. My grandparents greeted me at the door. My hand acting as a respirator shielded my nose from the stench. No-No commented, "I was like you, hating that smell. I'm used it. It's almost as if I don't smell it anymore. Yous East End girls, let me tell you, yous are too sensitive. Come on in before you pass out."

I couldn't bear the stench surging from the Steel Plant stacks. I always loved the city's East End, further away from the Plant. My monthly visits to see my grandparents hadn't made me any more used to that smell.

No-No had lived in the West End for her entire life. She had grown to ignore the reek of rotten eggs.

April 1, 1932. No-No was born in Sault Ste. Marie. My great-grandparents called her "Norma," but as she grew, her name transitioned into "No-No." She was too outspoken, crass, and troublesome for her given name. Norma was a common first name in the 1930s. No-No was far from common or ordinary.

As a young girl, No-No played dominoes with

the boarders. She hustled them out of their drinking money. Anichka became angry with her daughter, "No-No, no, this stops. Now! Yeah taking food right out of your brother's and sister's mouths." No-No didn't stop. She swindled enough money out of the boarders to purchase a dark blue 1940s Regal Gumball Machine. She set it up in the front room by the pool hall in that three-storey boarding house. Billiard players received two gumballs for five cents. No-No stored the coins she earned under her bed, a practice she'd learned from Anichka.

I stood in my grandparents' cramped living room. No-No had recounted the story of how she came to own the gumball machine. She had begun to search the room for it. "I'm sure it's here somewhere. I'm sure I kept it. See it? Sheila?"

I peered around the living room. My eyes couldn't focus on one item out of the plenty. I saw rolling hills of antiques and garbage twisting through the living room. "No, Grandma, I don't see a gumball machine."

Perhaps she did still own that gumball machine, along with the hills of other collectibles that she'd gathered over many years. Her house was filled with such treasures. No-No was a collector.

She kept rummaging through years' worth of collecting and buying. "I know I still...I'm sure I kept it."

Ollie, who had left the house in spite of the brewing storm, returned with a birthday cake for his wife. Grandmother wanted to cut the cake right away, but we had nowhere to sit and enjoy it. Everything in the house was buried. The kitchen table was hidden under glass ornaments, wood sculptures, Indian artifacts, antique purses, vintage hats, fermented Avon products, and taxidermy. It was all decaying, inside that overstuffed home.

We couldn't all sit on the La-Z-Boy, the sole available seat in the house. All other seating was beneath an assortment of detritus that some would call "junk." We could have eaten the cake outside on the picnic table, but the rain persisted into the evening.

Giving up on the cake, Grandmother recommenced searching for her gumball machine. "I know it's here. Somewhere."

I sat on the dusty La-Z-Boy. A television was positioned against the far wall over the hills and through a valley of antiques. To my surprise, the television still worked. Fortunately, my grandparents hadn't lost the remote, otherwise they would have no other way to reach beyond the collectibles to manually change the channel.

Still rummaging, No-No paused to ask, "How about this? Do you like this? It's really old. I'll give it to you. As long as you promise not to gift it to one of your friends." She had selected a piece of jewellery from one of her piles and offered it to me. "On second thought, maybe, maybe not, not today, I've lots of jewellery, we can go through it another time and you can pick out something you like, but not today, today isn't good, too much going on in celebration of my birthday." She replaced the piece of jewellery atop another random pile in the living room.

No-No's favourite words included "old," "vintage," "collectible," "collector's item," and "a real antique."

I kissed her on the cheek. "It's you who should be getting presents today, Grandma." But I didn't have a birthday gift for her. She had everything. I didn't know what to buy her. "I thought a visit would be nice."

She continued to dig through her collectibles. She was not about to give up her search for that gumball machine. No-No talked to me while she searched, "I'm curious. How was lunch with your great-aunt the other day? Did Juanita have anything ready for your mom and you's visit? Did she make yous anything to eat?"

"We had a nice time. Juanita made cake, dessert squares, and tea."

"Really? How many cakes were there? How were the desserts? Disgusting? What did yous talk about? Did Juanita mention me? Did your mom have a good time? You know it's only right Juanita offered yous something, seeing how yous rarely get together and all."

"There was one cake. Four different types of dessert squares. They were delicious. Mom had a nice time. We talked about this-and-that. No, you weren't mentioned. Juanita did bring up Anichka." I tried to stand up from the La-Z-Boy, but I kept slipping back into it.

"Really? Why? What did she say? Juanita was always our mother's favourite. I can tell you stories. I can probably remember more than she does. Juanita is eighty-six, you know? Your great-grandma was a hard woman. With eight children, a boarding house, pool hall, and bar to look after, she had to be hard."

"What do you mean 'hard'?"

"She was a hard woman." Repetition was how No-No explained herself.

All of Grandmother's sisters had the same eyes. No-No had them too, indecipherable dark eyes. Eyes that absorbed light, projected almost no emotion even when laughing or crying. No-No rarely cried, but once in a while she'd smile.

I hugged and kissed her. "Happy birthday, Grandma. You know I love you, right?" She hugged me back and smiled.

I stumbled while walking through the alley of collectibles lining the hallway to the front door. Grandmother continued searching for that dark blue 1940s Regal Gumball Machine. I drove back to my apartment in the East End. As I drove, the reek of rotten eggs dissipated. I took my usual route travelling past the pillar on Queen Street West. As I passed, I waved to Anichka.

Lemon Bundt

I was thirteen and sitting at Great-Aunt Juanita's dining room table, and so was my mother. In the adjacent living room, Juanita's husband Murray lounged on the sofa.

Great-Aunt Bernie sat perfectly upright in the dining chair across from me. Her back didn't touch that of the chair. Her rigid posterior reminded me of a ballerina. She wasn't dainty enough to be a ballerina, though. She wasn't dainty at all for that matter. She didn't have the body, nor the soft face for it. Her name, "Bernie", was even too harsh for that profession.

Growing up, I didn't dream of becoming a ballerina. I knew no such person could exist in my city of Sault Ste. Marie. Arts and culture could never take firm root in our industrial soil and breathe in our cancerous air. As a Saultite, I'd have to have other aspirations.

Bernie was a housewife, so were Juanita and Mother. They were wives and mothers and nothing more. Years ago, Bernie married Great-Uncle Oskar who was Juanita and No-No's brother. Then retired,

Oskar had worked at the Steel Plant.

Bernie attempted to smile at me. Her lips curved upward, her teeth showed, her cheekbones higher than when her face was blank. The facial expression could have hardly been called a "smile." I smiled back at her, imitating how she had done it. She nodded, so I knew I'd smiled correctly. I'd been courteous but not excessively so. I'd learned from a young age that greetings in my family were done out of formality, not based on goodwill. Our greetings included: a quick wave, smile, nod, glance in one's direction, or a momentary slowing of pace in recognition of another's presence. During the ages when I'd learned to read and write, I also acquired the necessary skills to interpret and employ those familial gestures and mannerisms. More than anything, I mastered a quickness of wave. It performed like so:

1. *An upward movement of the forearm and hand.*
2. *Count for two seconds.*
3. *Return motion, replacing the arm parallel to the side of the body.*

All women on my mother's side favoured that form of greeting. I guess it was tradition.

In the living room, Great-Uncle Murray scratched lottery tickets. Juanita scolded him for making a mess on her sofa. Most of my relatives, including the great-aunts, had one pristine room in their house. It was called "The 'Good' Living Room." They'd use those rooms when important company visited. Otherwise good living rooms weren't to be entered unless my great-aunts were cleaning them. That was the unspoken rule. Those rooms reminded me of porcelain dolls, something like dainty ballerinas.

Juanita bought me a porcelain doll once to be nice. Mother wouldn't let me play with it. It was too fragile, too beautiful. I didn't care to touch the doll anyway. I had to be careful with her. Mother would've been angry if I'd dirtied the doll's crème-coloured dress or scratched her milky skin. I preferred to play with wooden blocks. I'd stack them, building the tallest tower that I could before it crashed on my bedroom floor. As a kid, I couldn't play in the good living room. Mother didn't allow such an intrusion.

For some reason that day, Murray was allowed to be in Juanita's good living room. He was allowed to sit on one of the plastic-covered sofas. He was allowed to scratch his lottery tickets upon it. I remember wondering if it was Murray's birthday. I thought, *Is that why he's playing in the 'good' living room?*

Even with permission, which was unlikely to be given, I was frightened of stepping foot into that room. I'd edge along the border of the room to reach the hallway, and then to the bathroom. Even at age thirteen as I was at that time, I was too intimidated to address Great-Aunt Juanita. I wished to ask if it was in fact Murray's birthday. But I didn't ask. Not Great-Aunt Juanita. I couldn't.

Relaxing in the good living room, Murray seemed unreachable even by sound. In the dining room, I sat in a narrow wooden chair. It had no cushion to soften the sit.

Bernie's face gave its typical smile in Juanita's direction. Bernie was directing her comment to Juanita. Bernie's face emptied of expression. She then had enough facial capacity to move on to speaking, "We didn't have television sets."

Juanita nodded. Mother nodded. I nodded.

Mother smiled quickly at Bernie and said, "When I was young, only a kid really, No-No bought our first Frigidaire. She charged it to our account. Father would go to the store and pay the bill in installments. The refrigerator was a beauty, all shiny and white, that Frigidaire."

Juanita and Bernie murmured in agreement and sipped on their tea.

Murray shouted from the good living room, "I worked at the Steel Plant like all men did back then." I imagined a thick layer of plastic wrapped the entire room and secured it from unimportant guests like me. It was like the same plastic covers on the sofas. Murray's voice popped the invisible bubble that protected the room.

No one seated at the table faced in Murray's direction. Bernie looked at Juanita and stated, "Back then, women could get jobs easy enough." Bernie lifted her teacup to her mouth, almost as if in triumph. She'd silenced Murray. She returned her cup to its saucer without taking a sip. "They were good jobs too. I'd walk along James Street, and I knew I could get a job at any one of those shops. Easy."

Juanita poured more tea into Bernie's cup and refitted the cozy over the pot. "The Depression changed things. Relief supported so many families in the Sault. Back then, there was no employment insurance like nowadays. Remember Bernie, those vouchers our families received, used to buy necessities like groceries?"

Murray's gruff voice erupted from the living room, "My family never went on Relief. During the Depression, my father worked one day a week. That was all the work he could find in this city. It was a pride thing. We got through it, without vouchers, without help, from anyone."

Juanita offered lemon Bundt cake to the women. I ate the parts of the cake with icing on it and left the rest on my plate. The icing tasted so sweet compared to its lemon counterpart, the cake. Bernie smiled at my plate and then at Juanita. Juanita tapped a fork on her own plate. "No waste, Sheila. During the Depression, I would have loved for such treats in front of you." Bernie smiled. Juanita smiled back at her. My own mother smiled at both of them. I finished the remaining lemon cake on my plate, even the parts without the icing. I hoped for no more Bundt.

As I admired my empty dish, Murray swore at his lottery tickets, "God damn it!"

The sun coursed through the kitchen window and created a spotlight on Juanita's hands. The light spun rainbows from the diamond rings on her fingers. She waved aggressively toward the good living room. She and her hands shouted, "Murray! That's enough. The entire neighbourhood doesn't need to hear how you're wasting all of *my* money."

"Your money? I'm using *our* money and having a bit of fun instead of saving for rainy days or saving this godforsaken living room for special occasions. For God's sake, we're in our seventies. What's the point of saving anything? I'm going to use *our* money and this living room while I'm still alive. Certainly can't use them when I'm dead." Murray's laughter seemed to echo through the living room and into the kitchen. I imagined a great gust of wind causing the women's tea cups to shake, Great-Aunt Juanita's bone china tea cups rattling against their matching saucers.

That dispute was the first time I'd heard family members show real emotion in front of other people, especially the relatives. In our family, no one wanted to lose face. Mother always told me that losing face gave other family members ammunition to fire at you and at will. She would say, "Keep your mouth shut. And your ears open."

Now that Great-Uncle Wasyl had died, old issues about Anichka's will resurfaced.

It was Bernie who took up the topic of the will. She served the women platters of accusations. I remember how her face burned red. She kept drinking tea to cool herself. Then she set her tea cup on its saucer with precise deliberation. "Now listen everyone, Oskar attended the reading of the will. He heard what was said. And as the executor, Juanita, you've been doing a great job. But something's wrong. Why is No-No still angry at you after all these years? There has to be a reason. You were close before this whole affair with the will. Sometimes I wonder why,

Juanita, you became executor after Wasyl's passing. You're the next oldest in the family, but surely the responsibility should have gone to my Oskar. He's the next eldest male. Now I'm only saying this because Oskar wants me to, he deserves that responsibility to be executor to his mother's will. I'm sure Anichka would have wanted it that way, for him to be executor after Wasyl's passing. She probably didn't want to deal with the fuss of altering the chain of command or something like that. Now I'm not sure how all this legal stuff works. But I'm sure it was the lawyer who advised Anichka about who should be the executor to the will and the successor to that position.

"What I'm trying to say is, that it's no one's fault per se. It's just that my Oskar deserves to be executor. Just like my Oskar deserves a family burial plot. Anichka bought seven plots for her remaining children. And as far as I know, you haven't assigned a single plot to anyone, right? You haven't, have you? We're all getting up there in age. Surely our children deserve some security. They deserve to know Oskar and I are taken care of. That we have a burial site, each."

At the time, Bernie was age seventy-one. Even with that, her voice betrayed anxiety. Her crow's feet affected her face when anger spewed out allegations.

Juanita relaxed at the head of the dining table. She adjusted the rings on her fingers. I remember wondering if she could see her reflection in those outsized diamonds.

She restored a sense of decorum but retained

her position of superiority by pouring more tea and changing the topic. "I don't know where Norma inherited her need to shop from, definitely not from me or my side of the family." Even though I wasn't knowledgeable about our family history at that time, it occurred to me that No-No was part of Juanita's side of the family. I wondered why they couldn't get along. Instead of asking questions, I cut a piece of lemon Bundt and pushed it into my mouth.

Juanita glared at me. "My cake must be good," she said. "It makes some people forget their manners. Appetite over etiquette. What's this world coming to?" Her words were sharp, just like the blade of her silver beaded cake knife. "It seems that Sheila, here, has inherited her grandmother's bad manners. Probably Norma's penchant for rummaging through garage sales has also been passed down." Juanita nodded at Bernie.

Bernie nodded at Juanita and added, "It seems that Sheila has inherited Norma's hunger for indiscriminate shopping."

Juanita smiled smugly, and took charge in changing the topic again. "You know Anichka was something of a bootlegger in the city. After closing time in the bar, she'd pour back any alcohol that remained in customers' glasses into the liquor bottles for the next day. Murray says that my family history is nothing to be proud of. I am proud. After all, that's how my family survived the Depression. 'It was a pride thing.'" Juanita mocked the words that Murray had spoken earlier in the conversation. She imitated his gruff voice. Then she cleared her throat and resumed speaking in her dignified tone. "When I was a young woman, a child, shots cost twenty-five cents at our boarding house, and while Norma visited the theatre, I was the one at home, cleaning. The few times I got to see a film, my father came and removed me from the theatre. I had to return home to clean and cook for the boarders. Norma doesn't know what hard work is. She might say she does—," Juanita paused and secured the last piece of lemon Bundt for herself.

"Wasyl and Oskar were in charge of keeping a close eye on the boarders. They collected the rent at the end of every week. Most boarders didn't stay with us long. They had to move with the trains. Alfred, the second eldest in our family, was often too sick to help. With him it was always one thing or another. Anichka told us that he had the same illness as Caesar, same as Lenin, and Dostoyevsky. Our neighbours called Alfred 'a lunatic.' We weren't sure why. Anichka never explained what they meant. The neighbours said the devil's finger touched him."

When I look back at that conversation now, I'm surprised by how much it revealed about our family history. I didn't realize it then. Just like I didn't fully realize that Juanita was never one for diplomacy. She would go on too long. "As you may already know, Norma was the housekeeper. She never did any housework though. One way or another, she got out of doing her chores. The third youngest, Audrey, helped in the kitchen when I was too busy. Audrey also learned to make soap out of lard for the family.

43

The youngest, Ruby and Brucie, were too little to help. They mostly got in the way."

I met Juanita's eyes and then nodded. I felt she needed to know I believed her. I was listening. Murray was listening too, somewhat. He returned the conversation to the topic of the cinema. He wanted to share his experience of going to see a film. "When I was a lad, I used to go to the movie theatre with only fifteen cents. It cost ten cents to see the film and five for a soda."

Mother attempted to shift the discussion away from the cinema and childhood memories. "Juanita, it's said you were born on the kitchen floor and maybe that's why you're such a good cook and baker."

Juanita laughed. I remember feeling relieved to hear laugher. Up until that moment, the visit to Juanita and Murray's house could have been described as "sour," like Great-Aunt's lemon Bundt.

After that fleeting moment containing one laugh, a smile lingered on Juanita's face. I counted the seconds that the smile endured. It was like a solar eclipse, rarely seen.

Juanita's smile remained even as she asked, "Who says that? I have never heard that before. It might as well be true. I'm not fond of cooking. I do it for my family. Some people say I have a good touch though."

Years later, I still think of Juanita whenever someone serves me Bundt cake. I remember that phenomenon of a smile.

Now that I'm older, I realize that not everything everyone says is entirely accurate. No-No had a different story, and she wasn't there to defend herself that day. At least part of Juanita's version of the past was true. No-No's house was packed with treasures she had found at endless garage sales. Perhaps the frugality of youth had shaped her.

Not long after Grandmother's eighty-second birthday, I visited my grandparents' house. Ollie fussed about in the backyard tool shed. No-No asked me about work at the library and without waiting for an answer started reminiscing about her own past. "People think they work hard these days, but it was tough when I was a kid. I cleaned all the boarders' rooms at our house. That was my chore. It was hard work. Took me hours to cleanse those eight bedrooms, not to mention the bathrooms. Those bathrooms were filthy. Floors covered in mud from the men's boots. Those men trucked everyday through the mucky railyard. Then, they brought their work home with them on their boots, not to mention their oily clothes tossed everywhere. The oil came off the trains and other machines the men fixed. Dirt and oily marks were everywhere. And I can't forget about the liquor bottles scattered around the rooms. Your great-grandma expected me to inform her whenever I'd discovered liquor bottles in boarders' rooms. She didn't permit outside alcohol to enter her house. She lost out on profits that way. She had her own bar to run, and money to make. The worst was when some of the men pissed in the sinks in their bedrooms. They were too lazy to walk down the hall to the communal bathroom for the boarders on the third floor."

"At what age did you start cleaning the boarders' rooms?"

"Young."

"How young?"

"Must've been around six years old. Your great-aunts and uncles and I had to help run the family business. Great-Grandma needed us to keep the place running. Good thing she had lots of children to staff that boarding house."

"You were cleaning rooms at six years old?"

She shrugged. "That was the way it was at our house. That was the way it was back then. A family worked together to get things done and survive. Juanita helped with the cooking and tidied our family's bedrooms on the second floor. And I mean this, she never had to work as hard as I did. I can tell you that right now. Let me tell you, Juanita had to clean a couple bedrooms, whereas I had eight rooms to make spotless, oh, and the boarders' bathroom, and clean the third floor hallway, and the stairs between the floors…"

Making Allowances

It began when Shadyn was ten. I was nine. It ended when I was ten. Shadyn was eleven.

My sister and I loved visiting a local candy store. It was two blocks from our childhood home in the East End. A middle-aged couple operated the confectionary in the front half of their house. Where there should have been a sofa and television, there was a store counter and shelves.

At age nine, I was struck by the enormous size of one of the store owners, the husband. The counter-top reached just above his knees. To this day, I believe that man was a giant. Using tiny tongs, his large hands dug inside candy containers and filled brown paper bags with treats, five-cent sugary blue whales, yellow marshmallow bananas, two-cent chewies dusted in a sour coating, gummy bears in an assortment of colours, sticky wiggly worms, two-cent chocolate balls rolled in sprinkles. I devoured them all.

Until. Mother said Shaydn and I couldn't buy any more candy, not with money from her or Father's wallet. We had to learn the value of a dollar.

I remember thinking, *Learn the value of a dollar? But I only need a few cents to buy candy.* Mother was set on teaching a new life lesson. In order to earn her weekly allowance, Shadyn's chores included washing and drying the dishes every night and on garbage day taking the trash to the street curb. My torture amounted to twice a week vacuuming the entire house, upstairs and downstairs. I thought working in the dark basement was chore enough; however, every morning, I had to make the family's beds. We received two dollars a week for our labour. Every Saturday night before bedtime, Mother would place the money on each of our pillows. On those nights, our minds rested easy; the work week was over for those eight hours when Shadyn and I slept.

Sunday evenings the entire family strolled to that local candy store, two blocks from our house. Shadyn and I were allowed to spend some of our hard-earned allowance. Mother made us save the rest of our earnings. She said, "Save some of your money. You never know." I wondered, *You never know, what? What do I need to know now?* I thought my mother made absolutely no sense. For a year, Shadyn and I completed our chores, earned our weekly allowance, spent a portion of the profits on candy, and saved the rest in ugly, large, pink, plastic piggy banks. Those piggy banks were another of Mother's great ideas. She explained that Shadyn and I needed somewhere to store our savings. Though they were her idea, Mother had forced us to purchase our own banks. The money had come out of our allowance. We had to save for weeks to have enough coin to pay for Mother's great idea. The value of Mother's lesson never seemed to end.

What did end was our weekly allowance. No-No put a stop to that nonsense, as she saw it.

It was another Saturday evening. Shadyn and I were excited for what awaited us at bedtime, only a few hours away. Our weekly earnings would create a dimple in each of our pillows. No-No had come over to visit our mother. It was one of Grandmother's rare visits to the East End. That morning, she had gone to countless garage sales in hope of purchasing more antiques.

When it came to garage sales, No-No would travel anywhere in the city to see what other locals were selling. She'd say that attending garage sales gave her a rare view into strangers' lives. She'd get to see what Saultites had bought, what things had made up their lives and filled their homes, stuff that people had thought were important, junk that'd once been of value but now was no longer needed. Those antiques would be the junk that No-No collected. She'd rename it her "Treasure."

On that particular Saturday evening, Mother and Grandmother sat at the kitchen table. I was there as well. Father was in a nearby room. Shadyn played in her bedroom down the hallway. No-No showed off her treasures to Mother. At garage sales that morning, No-No must've purchased something really exciting. She had no other reason to visit, certainly not to see us. We weren't that type of family, loving. She held up some object. I remember thinking No-No's treasure

49

didn't seem exciting. Her antiques were boring to my nine-year-old self. She hadn't bought any toys, nothing that made loud noises, nothing that whistled or banged, nothing that was colourful, nor anything that sparkled. No-No's treasures seemed like trash to me. Her trash covered the kitchen table.

From the nearby room, Father yelled into the kitchen, "Get that junk out of my house!" He stomped down the hallway and slammed my parents' bedroom door.

Mother looked blankly at No-No. "Don't mind him. He's tired. He got off nightshift at the Plant. He's just tired."

"Don't worry. I put up with the same thing with your father when he worked at the Plant. Good thing he's retired, your father's more easygoin'. Thank God. He'll put up with anythin'."

I leaned over and rested a hand on Mother's knee. "Mommy, remember what tonight is, right? Me and Shadyn get our allowance, right? Mommy? We done our chores. Tonight, right? Mommy? Right?..Mommy?"

"Yes, tonight. Now go play with your sister."

I left the kitchen. Instead of going to Shadyn's bedroom, I sat hidden in the hallway and listened to my mother and grandmother's conversation. Most of the time, I couldn't really understand grown-up chatter, but I did enjoy listening. It all seemed so secretive.

No-No asked Mother, "What's this about a weekly allowance? I've never heard of such a thing."

"The girls complete weekly chores. On Saturday night, Jon and I pay them a small amount for their hard work. We're teaching our girls about responsibility, that nothing in this world is free. It's a good life lesson."

"When I was young, let me tell you, we had chores. We worked hard. But we never expected to be paid for it. My brothers, sisters, and I, we were expected to do our chores when asked and to do them well. And do you think we were patted on the back for it? No."

"Jon and I run our household a little different than you did and Anichka did before you. Nowadays things are different, but we are instilling the same values in our girls."

"Chores are chores. They don't come with allowances. Put a stop to this, capiche? No allowances, and that's final."

"That didn't work back with Ronnie and it's not going to work now. Jon and I like rewarding our girls for their work."

"The girls do chores. They help around the house. And yes, when they're older, they can get jobs and start earning their own money. But for now, they have a responsibility to help out the family. That's the way it is and has always been."

"Times change, but it seems you don't. Jon and I are going to run our household the way that is best for our family."

"I can see parenting is going to take you some time. Look at you, your brothers and sisters, yous ended up okay. Didn't yous? I said moving to the East

End wouldn't be good for you. I knew this would happen."

"That what would happen?"

"You'd turn soft."

I heard No-No starting to pack her collectibles and she soon left.

Next morning, Mother asked Shadyn and I to come into the living room. She explained that we would still be completing our chores but we wouldn't receive a weekly allowance anymore. Mother said she was being too soft on us. With the end of our weekly allowance, so too was the end of our family visits to the neighbourhood candy store.

At age twenty, I finished my second year at the local university. I was studying to be an archivist. I worked part-time at a Tim Horton's coffee shop. I saved enough money to buy my first junky car. It was the first of many junkers that I'd own throughout my adulthood. In a year's time, Shadyn would graduate from the local college. She would become a Registered Nurse and move anywhere that wasn't our small and dull Northern Ontario city. Mother was still a stay-at-home mom. Father still slaved away, working tirelessly at the Steel Plant and daydreaming about retirement. He had a couple years before those dreams could become reality. By that time, Grandfather had been retired from the Plant for at least twenty years. He spent his time browsing the aisles at Canadian Tire, re-arranging his tool shed, visiting our family cabin on Lake Superior, booking yet another doctor's appointment for a check-up, doing blood work tests for this-or-that, and sleeping, and napping. After raising four children and countless student boarders, No-No stopped working all together. She focused on her hobby, collecting. Every Saturday, she drove around the city to shop for antiques at garage sales.

It was a Monday afternoon. I had been continuing the same ritual for two years, visiting my grandparents at their house about twice a month. I considered myself a "good" granddaughter. I tended to visit my grandparents on Mondays. They called that weekday, "Their Down-Day." On those days, my grandparents stayed at home and relaxed. Grandmother said retirement was exhausting sometimes. I wasn't certain if she was joking or not. Probably not. No-No took "down-days" very seriously.

In front of the detached garage, No-No lounged on a lawn chair and remarked on the day's warmth. She peered down the driveway and watched for movement in the neighbourhood. That was her Monday occupation. After I'd parked my junker, I sat in the empty chair beside No-No. That chair was usually reserved for Ollie. He was currently napping on his faithful La-Z-Boy in the house.

Grandmother and I surveyed the neighbourhood. I asked, "See anything interesting around the old place?"

She answered using her typical colloquialism, "Let me tell you—this morning, the mailman came by the house to deliver more bills. Property taxes are due. Later some kids biked past. My neighbour walked by and said 'hello.' I think she was on her lunch break. She works at a real estate company in town. She always comes home for her lunch break. She has to let her dog out to go to the bathroom. She owns a big dog, tall ugly thing. It probably tears up the house while she's at work. She's the neighbour who lives over there." No-No pointed to her neighbour's house.

"That's very interesting. Sounds like a busy day. Did you leave the house at all? Go out anywhere? Shopping or something?"

"Not today, Sheila. It's Monday."

"Down-Day."

"You got it."

"So what have you been up to?"

"You're looking at it." No-No patted the arms of her chair.

I smiled. "Actually I came over today for a specific reason. Could you tell me about Anichka and her illegal bar? In the past, I heard some family members mention your mother and her bar. I've always been curious about how she lived."

"I guess you're old enough to hear about such things. What you want to know?"

"What was it like growing up in that three-storey boarding house?"

"Back then, there were lots of boarding houses in the city. They were more common than in today's times. What was it like? It was hard work. Your great-grandma was strict but a good woman."

"Yeah?"

"Yes, she was a good woman. She stayed at home and ran the businesses, the boarding house, pool hall, and the bar downstairs. She got mad sometimes, but when you have eight children that tends to happen. And your great-grandpa used to drink, so he was also a handful along with us kids. Great-Grandma had lots of shifty characters to deal with, men visiting the bar. Those men, drunk, and hanging around the house. Sometimes it wasn't nice living there. But there was always excitement happening. It was like those Al Capone days. Have you heard of him? Al Capone had nothin' on your great-grandma Anichka," No-No smirked. "She was arrested a couple of times. The police caught her selling alcohol illegally. While she was in jail, Great-Grandpa had to keep care of the businesses, as well as my seven brothers and sisters and me. There was no one else to do it. Great-Grandma was locked up. My older brothers and sisters tried to help, but it was Great-Grandpa who had to step into Anichka's shoes. He had to be the grown-up. But he didn't know what he was doing. He fed my younger siblings sour milk in their baby bottles. The milk had gone so bad that chunks clogged the teat. My brothers and sisters cried from hunger. Great-Grandpa couldn't stand the noise. He left them in their high-chairs and went into the basement bar to serve drinks, and have a few himself." No-No became silent. More of her neighbours walked past on the sidewalk. We waved politely.

No-No and I sat looking down the driveway. We both waved at whoever strolled by. When Ollie had risen from his nap and came outside, I gave him his seat beside Grandmother. I kissed them on their foreheads and then drove home in my junky car.

Later in my diary, I wrote down the afternoon's events. Time. Setting. No-No's childhood memories. Image of spoiled milk. Spoiled image of my great-grandfather.

In the late-1980s, Anichka passed away. As a result, No-No became a wealthy woman. All of Anichka's seven living children were well-looked after following their mother's passing. She'd earned thousands from running the boarding house and illegal speakeasy. With that money, Anichka would support her family for years after her death.

Including No-No, each of Anichka's children had a different version on how the inheritance money was distributed. Most agreed that Anichka's money was divided evenly between her children. No-No took her portion of that inheritance money and separated it into three even piles. She stored each pile in three different accounts in three different banks around the city. She feared that one bank might "go under" and take her money with it. When it came to matters of money, No-No trusted no one, not even her family. Especially not them. Relations were just as sly as strangers. Only No-No had access to her three bank accounts. Ollie was told about the accounts but didn't have access to them. No-No put a little somethin' away on the side for herself.

Throughout their lives, No-No and Ollie lived off his wages from the Steel Plant and later in their elder years, they survived on his steel worker's pension.

No-No didn't save her inheritance for those rainy days as she would have done in the past. Then a rich woman, she began spending her fortune at garage sales, church bazaars, auctions, thrift shops, Value Village and Salvation Army stores. She bought her collectibles. Things accumulated in her house. She always found a place to store her latest purchase, though. Even when the house, tool shed, backyard, family cabin, boathouse, and even outhouse were full, No-No still found spaces in those buildings to pile her antiques.

No-No would visit a garage sale and spend some of her inheritance money on a used item. She would adore her latest purchase for a few hours, admire it, find a place to store it, and forget all about it. After those few precious hours, individual objects became part of the mass consuming space and my grandparents' lives. No-No forsook the comfort of their lives, the liveability of their home, and general necessities like a working stove, fridge, sink, bathtub, water heater, even relationships with family members—all for stuff.

As the piles of collectibles grew, the sum in No-No's three bank accounts dwindled. Until there was only a small savings left in one account.

Starting at a young age, I overheard my parents arguing about No-No's collecting hobby. Their anger unnerved the house. I hid in my bedroom and tried to plug my ears. Their arguments always sounded the same. Same issue. Same stern words.

Father would complain about No-No. He'd shout, "Her collecting, it has to stop. Your mother is out-of-control."

Mother would argue, "What am I supposed to do about it? She's my mom. I can't control her any more than my dad can."

"Right, your father, he should have put a stop to this years ago, way before their house and cabin became uninhabitable. How can your parents live like that?"

"You don't understand. Growing up, Mom didn't have much. I guess she's making up for it now."

"And that's a good excuse? Back then, no one had much. Doesn't give her the right to hoard. Your mother's a hoarder. That's the truth, ain't it?"

"She's not a hoarder, just a collector."

"Izza, your mother is a hoarder. It's beyond collecting now. She can't get rid of anything. What's going to happen when your parents die? They're going to leave all that stuff. That's your inheritance? Who's going to clean up that mess?"

"Don't you think that's enough? I don't feel like talking about this right now."

"But when? When are we going to talk about it? When is your family going to face the facts?"

"I can't talk about this anymore tonight. I'm going to check on the girls. I wouldn't be surprised if Sheila doesn't sleep at all. You know how much she loves her grandma."

"God knows why."

"Enough."

Suspended Bodies

In her own diary, Mother had written *makes you wonder,* after the words, *Alfred in his tiny* suit. I wondered about her wonderment.

The way the past unfolded depended upon who told it. Everybody agreed on Great-Uncle Alfred's bad health though. There was something in Juanita's words that had struck me even as a teenager. Only years later did I understand the connection between Caesar, Lenin, and Dostoyevsky. Juanita's words about Alfred's hapless state echoed in Mother's diary. And Alfred emerged again as a shadow in a story Ollie used to retell. In the summertime, Grandfather would always be at camp, our family's simple cabin near Lake Superior. It would be too nice outside to be anywhere else, especially in the busy concrete city.

I was twenty-five and still driving the same junky car I had owned since I was twenty. By that time, the car had to have been thirteen years old at least. That rusty junker was hardly safe to drive within the city, let alone speeding on Highway 17, north of Sault Ste. Marie and descending the steep Mile Hill.

When I arrived at the family cabin, Ollie relaxed in a lawn chair, nursing a beer. I was happy to join him and drank a beer myself. My junker's engine, and my own anxiety about driving, were still hot.

Grandfather asked, "How was the drive?"

I took a long drink of beer.

"Going for a dip in the lake later?"

Even on the warmest of summer days, I could swim in Lake Superior and be numb from my ears to toes. In the summer or fall season, it didn't matter. Lake Superior was always cold.

I looked at the large body of water in front of me. "Perhaps I'll stick my toes in later and see how it is."

"Probably a good idea. When I was your age, even younger than you, I was forever going swimming, going to the beach or cooling off in a creek or pond. In the summer, swimming was our source of entertainment, me and the other neighbourhood kids. I remember when I was young, maybe around fifteen, some kids and I were swimming at Dean's Creek. I'm not sure why the creek was called that. Maybe we named it. That was our creek. All the neighbourhood kids went there. The creek was at the bottom of a five to six-foot embankment. We had to walk in a ways for the creek to be deep enough to swim in.

"I remember one time, me and the boys followed the oldest boy there. He was an all-round athlete and in the Sea Cadets. It was the summer of 1944. The oldest boy kind of liked to show off, figured he was in charge of us. That day, the oldest boy dove headfirst into the water. He didn't dive out far enough. His head hit the sand. He came up gagging for air. He couldn't move. We didn't know it, but he'd snapped his neck. I ran into the water and grabbed him. I held him up. His eyes were so big. Another boy went to call for help. Some of the kids and I carried him up the embankment. We were careful not to slip and drop him. We didn't know anything. We didn't know what else to do for him. We didn't know First Aid or anything like that. The kids and I laid him on the ground at the top of the embankment. All I knew was we had to get him out of the water so he didn't drown. An ambulance came across the farmer's field to where he was lying. The paramedics carted him off to the hospital. A couple days later, the oldest boy died.

"He was the only one to dive. The water was clear, but there was a clay ridge at the shore before the water got deep. Maybe he never saw the ridge, no way to know for sure. Us kids didn't know what he was thinking. He just didn't jump out far enough. Five or six of us were there that day, mixed gang of girls and boys. The oldest boy wasn't the only one who died young. There was Alfred too. He was your great-uncle, Anichka's boy. He was the second born after Wasyl. Alfred was a strong boy, not as small-boned as his older brother. Despite his strength, Alfred got really sick one day, had some kind of fit, was all paralyzed, kind of. Alfred died of complications by the time he reached thirteen."

It wasn't until I began investigating my family history that I learned why I'm an epileptic. Doctors couldn't pinpoint a direct cause. During childhood, I experienced some head trauma: falling off my bike, a neighbourhood kid throwing a baseball at me, maybe I was dropped on my head as a baby as the saying goes. I almost drowned once at the family camp. Shadyn saved me. Perhaps as I sank to the bottom of Lake Superior, I drank too much water. Perhaps all that water travelled to my head and shifted some things around up there.

After Grandfather had told me about Alfred's death, I read books on general seizure disorders.

Epilepsy is likely to develop if there's a family history of it. In many cases, heredity plays a role.

Since my first epileptic attack at age thirteen, I had four to five grand mal seizures and multiple petit mal fits. Since I was diagnosed thirteen years ago, I've been on medication. My disorder has been more or less under control. I always become uneasy, though, when I sense the aura of something coming.

Ollie dug into the cooler sitting beside him. He retrieved two more beers for us. "Years later, your grandma No-No told me all this: a small funeral for Alfred was held in the front room of the Vovk family boarding house. Streamers draped the ceiling. Twelve neighbourhood children played mandolins around the casket, two rows on either side. Alfred was displayed in an open coffin cushioned with plush cream fabric. Alfred's hands rested on his chest. Bundles of mixed flowers were arranged around his body. He wore a black suit and tiny bowtie. Your great-grandma

Anichka had bought the best suit available, off the rack at a local men's shop. She hung a large purple bow on the front door announcing a death in the family."

Thinking back to Ollie's account, I mixed the image of young Alfred in his lush casket with that of Oldest Boy, the wide-eyed young swimmer who gagged for life. Black suit. Tiny bowtie. Clear water. Clay ridge. Children swimming. Playing mandolins. Purple bows.

Mother used to recite family stories to Shadyn and I, but none about Alfred. I would overhear private conversations between relatives, few words here-and-there. Then with Ollie's help, I was able to piece together the story of Alfred.

The neighbours would call him 'a lunatic' and 'the boy who wasn't right.' They'd say things like he'd been touched in the head or by the devil's finger, he was crazy, or dangerous, and they wouldn't trust younger children around him. Alfred was rarely outside. He barricaded himself in the boarding house. Alfred was an epileptic like me. In those days, it seemed like people didn't want to listen or learn about his condition. Anichka always overheard neighbours gossiping, blathering, on the sidewalk. Inside the house, Alfred was having seizures. One of those attacks could have resulted in a head trauma. Maybe he fell on his head and nobody saw, internal hemorrhage. Perhaps no one knew the symptoms, the warning signs. Perhaps there were none. The bleeding contained and unseen on his body. That part of the story no one seems to know. How did Alfred die of epilepsy? Did he have a violent attack and stop breathing? All that's known is one day, Alfred died, and it's somehow connected to his epilepsy. What really happened is so close, yet so distant.

I read how years ago people thought epilepsy was caused by the supernatural. They thought epilepsy was caused by feeblemindedness, insanity, witchcraft, lack of religious faith, even demonic possession. They considered epilepsy to be a punishment for those who sinned against the moon and its goddess. Epilepsy was a bad omen. Epileptics were unclean, a disgrace. In ancient times, they spat at the sight of epileptics to ward off the disease. Even further back in time, then, people thought epilepsy was divinely inspired. I found a book by Hippocrates titled *On the Sacred Disease:*

> *It is thus with regard to the disease called Sacred: it appears to me to be nowise more divine nor more sacred than other diseases, but has a natural cause from the originates like other affections. Men regard its nature and cause as divine from ignorance and wonder, because it is not at all like to other diseases. And this notion of its divinity is kept up by their inability to comprehend it, and the simplicity of the mode by which it is cured, for men are freed from it by purifications and incantations.*

It seems some people are afraid of things they don't understand. They will invent divine or supernatural reasons for things they can't comprehend. Nobody seemed to understand what Alfred was going through. If I lived during his time, we could have talked about our condition.

The House Special

Below, in the basement of her boarding house, Anichka ran a makeshift bar selling liquor and beer. Her children weren't allowed in the bar until they were sixteen. Then, they were allowed to witness intoxicated men drinking to excess, spewing foul language, and breaking into fist-fights. Some of the older children knew what was going on in the basement. They were used to playing on the first floor and hearing the ruckus erupting from the bar, below.

The basement had no windows. A few tiny lamps lit up the bar. Amid mismatched furniture, tables, stools of various heights mixed with odd, wooden kitchen chairs, neighbours, family friends, billiard players, and boarders tried to forget the daily drudgery. Anichka had scavenged the furnishings from neighbours' lawns or the dump, woodwork scarred by broken glasses, festooned with dings, dents, ring stains.

It was in the days during the Prohibition that Anichka made her move into the business. The profits helped her family through the Depression.

My family doesn't know where Anichka got the

booze. Maybe she solicited bootleg alcohol from men living in outlying areas who made moonshine from illegal stills. "Bootlegging" for Saultites meant that homeowners sold alcohol in their homes. Locals called it, "Home Sell." Other Saultites supplied moonshine or bootleg liquor to illegal establishments.

After Prohibition ended, Anichka continued to run her illegal bar during the 50s and early-60s. She didn't have a liquor license, but she sometimes purchased alcohol legally. After Ontario repealed Prohibition in 1927, the Liquor Control Board of Ontario was founded. Anichka bought her supplies from LCBO stores and from a beer delivery service. Door-to-door salesmen employed by different brewery companies knocked on her door and asked how many cases of beer she wanted that week. Later her order would be delivered on the back step.

In the mid-1940s to 50s, "home sell" was common in Sault Ste. Marie. Though it was technically illegal, residents accepted the practice. It was considered normal because extra income was often needed by many families to survive. On any given street, there were houses that ran illegal bars.

What made Anichka's business different, successful, was her four daughters. When each daughter turned sixteen, entry into the bar became a rite of passage. Juanita was first to enter the speakeasy.

Every morning in the second level kitchen, Juanita brewed tea. On the stove, the batch cooled until that night. When six o'clock approached, she funnelled the tea into glass bottles and carried them into the basement. Male patrons whistled at pretty Juanita as she entered. They asked to buy a drink for Anichka's pretty daughter. Anichka poured dark liquor into one shot glass and the other she filled with the cold tea. The customer received the actual shot; Juanita received the tea. The man and Juanita slammed back their drinks. Somehow Juanita never got drunk. The men got a thrill each time, charged for two shots of alcohol. Anichka made her money. When the other daughters came of age, they joined Juanita. Together they bamboozled the men who didn't know it was all a ruse.

Anichka's bar was always crawling with drunken men, some passed out on tables. Among them, a woman who came to the bar every Friday night just after nine o'clock. Sometimes that woman brought Anichka bottles of homemade liquor. The woman used those bottles as currency, payment for her drinks. One bottle was worth two rounds of drinks for the next three Fridays. Each week, the woman's husband gave her a set amount of money for family necessities. The woman saved where she could, but sometimes there wasn't money left over to buy herself a drink. The homemade liquor she made was supposed to be for her husband's personal supply. She soon learned the advantages of selling moonshine on the side.

At first the woman brewed alcohol in large barrels in her kitchen, but her husband abhorred the stench of the fermenting ingredients and the way the smell permeated the kitchen along with the entire first floor of their house. One day the woman's husband retrieved a dirty clawfoot bathtub from the dump. He carried the tub to the attic for the woman to make her brew out of sight, if not out of mind. The woman scrubbed the bathtub clean. The liquor she brewed removed the remaining yellow ring from inside the tub. Onions, dandelions, goldenrods, anything the woman could find or spare from her pantry fermented in that bathtub.

When she received a bottle, Anichka diluted the homemade brew with a mixture of cheaper alcohol to be sold from the bar. In return, Anichka granted the woman credits for drinks.

Anichka sold the brew as the house special. She received that brew on rare occasions, which made it all the more desirable among customers. Anichka sold "the good stuff" for double the usual price, fifty cents per shot.

The woman's husband never purchased shots of the good stuff. It was too expensive for his taste and meagre wallet. And so, the husband never discovered that his wife sold bottles from his personal stock. And he never bothered to count the stock of moonshine in his pantry at home. He always grabbed a bottle, uncorked it, and left the pantry without taking notice.

The woman and her husband both visited Anichka's establishment but never at the same time. He didn't allow his wife at such a place. He thought it indecent for a woman to be drinking alcohol and unescorted in a public setting. Little did he know.

One day, so I've been told, unbeknownst to her husband, the woman relaxed in Anichka's bar, drinking a glass of beer. The woman always sat alone at the same table close to the stairs. Men surrounded her. They were laughing, shouting, spilling their drinks on the already sticky floor. Even with that noise, the woman's ears were attuned to the sound of her husband's heavy steps and breathing. His visits were frequent but irregular. The woman always had to beware of his presence.

The woman heard her husband coming. Through the stair railing, she saw his weighty work boots tramping, down, into the bar. The woman gulped the remainder of her beer, grabbed hold of her purse on the nearby seat, and slipped out the back entrance.

That woman, Oksana, was my grandfather's mother. Anichka was the bartender. Oksana was Anichka's best customer.

Anichka's daughter, No-No Vovk, eventually married Oksana's son, Ollie Salenko. Ollie and No-No's second oldest child was Izza, my mother. I remember how some relations would brag about our good stock.

Around age thirteen, Great-Grandmother Oksana and her family moved from Quebec to Sault Ste. Marie. Oksana's father, Aimery, came to work for the Algoma Central Railway. Months into his employment, Aimery met Andriy. He was a confident and smart-mouthed twenty-year-old railway worker. Andriy often visited Aimery's house to have supper with the family. That was when Andriy met Aimery's daughter. In 1922, Oksana and Andriy married.

If family lore was accurate, then a couple of years

into their marriage, Andriy's hard ways drove Oksana, devoted Catholic, to join in his love of liquor. Aimery always felt guilty for being the link that connected his daughter and Andriy.

Over the years, I gathered a description of my paternal great-grandfather. Andriy was "smart," "skillful," "hard," "drunk," "alcoholic," and "mean."

Only once do I remember my grandfather talking about Andriy. "My father was a head foreman for the ACR. Did you know that my father could fix anything? Loose tracks. Unhinged railings. Signal lights. Did you know my father had a job all through the Depression? And our family still had no money. My father drank away his pay. My father would take shots of whisky and chase them with beer. And later, my father would retire for the night with a bottle or two of vino. Empty bottles would accumulate around his bed. My father was a mean drunk. One year, all I received for Christmas was a single balloon. Red."

Loads and Laneways

It was March 28, 1938. A letter was published in an edition of the local newspaper, *The Sault Daily Star*. The letter was composed and mailed in by an anonymous Saultite. It was featured in the newspaper's "The Women's Page." In the letter, the nameless author described the scene, women visiting public beverage rooms, along with the type of 1930s woman who frequented such places, a confidently daring and yet respectable female for her time. That was the type of woman who the nameless author aspired to be like. The nameless female author signed her letter, "Envious."

AGAINST BARRING WOMEN FROM BEVERAGE ROOMS

Editor Sault Star Women's Page:
I've been reading quite a bit lately about closing up beverage rooms for women. Some women's clubs are going as far as sending in petitions to the government, asking them to close beer parlours to women.

For my part, I don't care for beer, but I don't see why the women who do like it, can't drink it out in public, the same as a man. Women nowadays stand along side of men almost anywhere. This generation isn't in Grandma's time, where women were afraid to go out and get a job, in those days women couldn't support themselves, and you'd never dream of seeing a woman sitting down to a glass of beer and a cigarette. It just wasn't done. But today when a woman is just as independent as a man, why shouldn't she go to a beverage room, and have a glass of beer? It helps quiet the nerves and she can relax a little after a busy afternoon.

Of course, I certainly don't believe that these places should be open to girls of 16 or 18. The woman who sits and drinks till she makes a fool out of herself, isn't to be compared with the respectable woman who will sit down for a drink and a chat and go about her business. And that last, is the kind of woman I envy. I would like to be like her, only I have too timid a soul. I hope some day to drink a glass of beer, and maybe smoke a cigarette (if it doesn't choke me), and feel that I'm not doing anything wrong.

ENVIOUS

Back in the 1930s, locals never saw a woman smoke a cigarette in public. It just wasn't done. Except Anichka, who stood smoking alongside men. She was the one serving the liquor. She was daring and somewhat respectable.

The late-1930s to early-1960s, Anichka's booze sales supplemented Nicholas' paycheques from the

Steel Plant. Because of her enterprise, Anichka was arrested several times. Policemen raided the boarding house searching for contraband liquor. Storming into the nursery, the police flashed lights in the children's faces. Their theory was that the most innocent place to hide alcohol was in the nursery. They weren't far off. Although they never discovered the stash, if they had looked under the rug in the nursery and lifted a large section of floorboard, there was a space between the ceiling of the first floor and hardwood flooring of the second. In that space, Anichka hid her liquor.

Discovery of a cache of contraband was the police's main goal, a big bust. In the absence of bust, and when they lost patience with Anichka's flagrant disregard of the law, they would enter the bar and file an arrest. On the first of many such arrests, they cuffed Nicholas instead of Anichka. It was improper to arrest a woman, wife, mother of eight young children. She demanded they arrest her; otherwise, Nicholas might lose his job at the Plant. The police consented. Anichka was imprisoned for a week and had to pay a ten dollar fine. She paid the same amount as other neighbourhood men who ran similar establishments. The men's offenses were recorded in the city's newspaper. Anichka's were not. Other people who came into contact with my family would also get in trouble with the law.

Last month, I visited my parents' house. I was tired of using the local laundromat and wanted to use my parents' washing machine. Mother was hanging garments on the clothesline outside. The autumn breeze was strong and smelled of the neighbouring pine. Mother retrieved one of Father's work shirts that had blown off the clothesline and re-pinned it on the wire. "Maybe it's too windy to be drying clothes outside today." We sat in lawn chairs and chatted while my load cycled through the washer.

Mother looked at me. "You know, my childhood was always busy and noisy and packed with people and daily chores and life. Your grandma boarded Indian boys from Moose Factory and Moosonee. The boys came to the Sault to attend high school. Your grandma was used to living with boarders because of her upbringing. She grew up in a boarding home, but I think you already know about that. I can never remember what stories I've already told you. When my brothers and sisters and I were kids, we'd visit Anichka's house every Sunday. She'd always have a package of cabbage rolls and perogies defrosting on the porch. That was one thing about your great-grandma, she would always have something to offer family when they visited. Very European, you see? Grandma would go inside the house and talk to Anichka while us kids would sit outside and eat our plate of perogies. Anichka was never chintzy when it came to food. When it came to money, then she was what we used to call a 'cheezler.'"

"'Cheezler'?"

"How can I explain this? She was always trying to make a buck, you see?"

"Guess so."

"It was Anichka who told No-No to take in boarders. Anichka gave the same old speech to everyone, your grandparents, aunts and uncles, even me. You would have probably received the same advice if she were still alive today. Anichka would say, 'Always have a little money put away on the side. Ya never know what'll happen.' No-No listened to her mother and boarded Indian boys to make extra money. The first load of boarders came when I was in the sixth grade. After that, we had five to nine more loads of three to four students at a time. Grandma requested to take in male boarders instead of females. She thought males washed their hair less and wouldn't drive up the water bill. No-No insisted males were less maintenance. I couldn't tell the difference."

No-No was cheap. Mother said it was because Grandmother grew up during the Depression. That's why No-No is the way she is. In those days, Saultites had to be cautious about their money. Lots of locals were out of work. People were poor. No-No, though, was different than other people her age. I always knew that. I just didn't know the word to describe her.

Mother continued, "Grandma made ninety dollars a month per student she boarded. The government made it so that the money any household made didn't affect their baby bonus. Grandma's baby bonus cheque was the same amount with or without boarding students. We didn't have to pay income tax on the money earned either. Necessities like aspirin, soap, and lice shampoo, our family received for free as a part of the house-family program. Those Indian boys were always coming down from Moose Factory and Moosonee with lice. Thank God, they didn't sleep in my room. My younger brother and sister and I slept in one bedroom. The Indian boys slept in the room down the hall. Lots of Indian boys slept in that room over the years like the Small Brothers, George and Gabe. The brothers hated each other so much they never talked."

"Never?"

"Never."

"Why not?"

"Family don't have to like each other. They don't always get along just 'cause they're related."

"Allen slept in the Indian boys' bedroom. Their room and mine had bunk beds. Otherwise those small rooms couldn't fit all of us. In my bedroom, the bunk bed could only fit if it ran along the wall with the closet so I couldn't use it. That was my dream though. Growing up, I always wanted a bedroom with a useable closet. It wasn't much of a dream but I always kept my wishes simple. Once, I wished that Grandma would change the weekly supper menu. That dream never happened, not with the mother I had. No, not with No-No. I can still remember what we had for each meal. Everyday for breakfast, she made porridge. It was either oatmeal, Cream of Wheat, or Red River cereal. My favourite was Red River. I used to love that stuff. Porridge was easy, meaning it was an inexpensive way to fill up our family and those Indian boys. She slapped together sandwiches for everyone's lunches including your grandpa's meal for work. She used to slice the Klik so thin I could see through it."

"What's Klik?"

"It's like Spam, luncheon meat in a can. It was disgusting. That's all you need to know. Grandma used the plastic bags bread came in to package our lunches. One Indian boarder went to the local university. He asked Grandma if he could have his sandwiches wrapped in wax paper. He was in university."

"Did she?"

"Yeah, she wrapped his sandwiches in wax paper, only *his* mind you. Every day, we had a different meal. That way, Grandma could buy food in bulk. Our family had soup on Sundays. Well, we had soup with every meal, lunch and supper. Grandma had to fill up those Indian boys somehow. On Sundays, we also had Shake'n Bake chicken, two pizza pans' worth, roast potatoes, and some type of canned vegetable. For dessert, Grandma made Jell-O, pudding, apple squares, or raisin bars. We always had some type of dessert. She had to bribe us to eat our suppers. Us kids always looked forward to dessert, but it was never very good. It was better than the supper though. Grandma was never a very good cook or baker. Not like Juanita, no comparison. On Mondays, Grandma prepared meatballs and gravy with boiled potatoes. Wednesday was spaghetti night. The spaghetti sauce was somewhat of a concoction. It was a blend of two cans of Bravo sauce and two cans of tomato soup. As you can imagine, it was runny. I can't remember what we had on the other days. You can call Grandma later and ask. She might remember."

"Pork chops, maybe? On Tuesdays?"

"No. No. Too expensive. It was anything cheap. Oh. And my place at suppertime wasn't at the table with everyone else. Grandma used to pull out the silverware drawer of a large cabinet we had in the dining room. She'd place a wood cutting board across the open drawer. I'd retrieve a stool from the kitchen. And that would be my own little spot at supper."

"So you didn't enjoy living with boarders?"

"Not really. It meant Grandma wasn't able to come to the family cabin on the weekends. She had to stay home and take care of the Indian boys. She was too busy. Your grandpa, aunts and uncles, and I went to camp without her. We spent some of our weekends there and our entire summer holidays. We lived at camp from the day school was out until the first day back. It didn't matter if Grandpa had just got off nightshift and was tired, he'd pack up the truck and head to camp. When Grandpa had to work, he'd travel the forty minutes from camp to the Sault. He'd work his twelve hours and come right back out."

"So you enjoyed your childhood?"

"Not particularly. I never had many friends growing up. The other neighbourhood kids used to walk past my house heading toward the basketball courts. They never stopped to get me."

"Why not?"

"Don't know. Even in high school, I didn't have many friends. I wasn't very pretty," Mother shrugged.

79

"And having the Indian boys around didn't help my popularity. No one else boarded students in our neighbourhood. Everyone knew about it too, except Grandpa's friends at camp. One day, it came out. I can't remember how. I think I accidentally said something in front of Grandpa's friend. Grandpa was angry with me. He was more embarrassed than anything. After that day, people knew."

"Did the Indian boys like living at your house? Did they like Grandma?"

"Hard to say. In their adulthoods, some of the Indian boys returned to visit Grandma."

"Really?"

"Oh yeah. Your grandma wasn't always good to them. Whatever happened at our house, it was always the Indian boys' faults. She called them 'chornys'... only when speaking with Anichka mind you."

"'Chornys'?"

"It's a slang word meaning 'black.'"

"Why use that word?"

"Maybe because they were darker-skinned? Grandma did have good relationships with the boys. She'd joke around with them and say things like, 'How'd ya get here, by canoe?' or 'Say, if you marry a Chinese woman, what colour would your children be?' Grandma would start laughing. You know that laugh of hers, the kind of mean-spirited one?"

I learned that sometimes Mother didn't mind having the Indian boys living in their already crammed house and taking up Grandma's time and attention. Sometimes even though the boys were older, they played with Mother and her younger sister and brother. Sometimes she thought the boys were fun because they weren't like Allen who ignored her and everything that wasn't relevant to his life.

One of the older Indian boys used to take Mother and her sister and brother for joyrides along the laneway behind their house. Like most laneways in Sault Ste. Marie, the one that ran behind Mother's childhood home had no street sign, no name. In everyday speech, locals aptly called it and other lanes, "The Lane," or "The Laneway," or "The Laneway Out Back," or "The Lane Out Back."

Tommy was the name of that particular older Indian boy, the joyrider. Tommy was different. Then thirteen, Izza noticed how most of the Indian boys who came through the house had slick, straight hair. Not Tommy. Tommy had kinky hair and a junky car, his first car. He'd cruise back and forth down along the laneway. It was too narrow to turn the car around so he'd coast back and forth.

During one joyride, the siblings squirmed in the backseat while Tommy drove. Back and forth, they drifted along the laneway until their ride was interrupted. The police stopped the car to ask for Tommy's driving license. It was inside the house. The police would've allowed Tommy to retrieve his license, but he never mentioned that he had one. He knew No-No didn't like police at the house from her days of growing up in the boarding house. She couldn't forget how the police had raided her childhood home with no concern for her safety and that of her younger siblings. She instructed the Indian boys, "No cops, coppers at your house ain't a good thing. Keep them away from here." Out of respect for her wishes, Tommy took the rap and was fined for driving without a license.

He spoke about it afterward, "It's because I'm Native. That's the only reason they stopped me. Lots of white kids drive without licenses. Those coppers saw my brown skin and wrote the ticket."

Untouched by Makeup

It was a day last June. I remember I spent it alone in the library searching through genealogical records and sketching my family tree, links between generations, wives to husbands, children to their children. I collected the findings in my diary. I ruminated on the links, all those marriages, how the lovers met.

It was 1950. No-No had short black hair then. It fell to her jaw line, pointing toward her darkly painted lips. Though her eyebrows were brushed with shadow, her already captivating eyes didn't need makeup.

In her late teens, No-No was still cleaning rooms at the boarding house. Her boyfriend Albert helped with some of the chores. He washed the floors and fixed small appliances. He helped with maintenance at the boarding house. To Anichka, Albert was "free labour." Albert was short, his face ingrained with hard lines, a blue-collar Humphrey Bogart. Bogie and Albert, both were not classically good-looking but they were leading men.

A year into their courtship, Albert passed away

from liver disease. He tried to conceal his condition from No-No, continuing to help out around the boarding house while he grew ill and thin. At his passing, No-No refused to cry.

Years later, Juanita told me how days after Albert's funeral, No-No cursed vehemently behind closed doors and threw objects against her bedroom wall. Juanita admitted Albert's death wasn't fair. Sitting at her dining room table that day, I was confused by Juanita's sympathy for No-No, confused by the sudden gesture of affection. "I couldn't relate to Norma's sadness. I tried. She was my sister, but I was already married to Murray. I was happy. I didn't want to think about how it might be to lose someone like that." Juanita told me how after Albert's death, No-No only left the house when she had to work at a local grocery store. Juanita's lips curved to reveal that rarely seen smile. "After one of her work shifts, Norma met Ollie while walking back to the boarding house."

Juanita's version on how my grandparents met was different from the way No-No recounted it. She would always tell the story of how she met her husband to be as thus: "He'd pick somethin' cheap off a store shelf. Cheap stuff for his lunch, I'd imagined. Anything really, anythin' just to get a glimpse of me. Ollie would peer down every check-out aisle looking for me. He'd pretend he needed that one little item for his lunch, but I knew better. He just wanted to talk to me. Let me tell you, I was a looker. No doubt about that. A looker. One day, he came to my till with a single can of tuna. He put a hundred-dollar bill on the counter. I wasn't impressed. He probably thought I would be. But I wasn't. See, I was a looker. Besides I wasn't even sure if I had change for a hundred. Ollie was twenty-one at the time. Rumour had it that since eighteen, he'd been working at the Plant. On our first date, he tried to impress me again by talking about his job. Ollie boasted how he'd worked in the Open Hearth during his first year at the Plant before he was transferred to another department. He said somethin' about how, 'That's where excess carbon and impurities are burnt out of pig iron to forge steel. The Open Hearth is hot and dangerous. I worked with boiling liquid metals.' He talked like that for hours. I made him court me for years before I gave in to marrying him. I was the catch, a looker. Didn't even wear a stitch of makeup. That's how much of a looker I was. Real pretty. You'd understand if you'd seen me. Not in photographs, but in person. A real looker. I was. Ollie was lucky to get me."

Ollie had another view. He always grinned before he gave his version. His emerald eyes smiled at me. "I shopped at that grocery store where your grandma worked. She'd always sneak a peek at me when she thought I wasn't looking. I caught her stares. I'd usually go through her line. She never spoke to me, not even to say, 'Here's your change.' I guess she was shy. I got the impression that she liked me. One day, Juanita called me to go on a double-date. Back then, everyone knew everyone. A couple days later, I parked my new 1950s two-tone Monarch Sport Sedan with a bold grille and a thick chrome surround—and walked up to the front door. Juanita and Murray were already there. Like me, Murray worked at the Steel Plant, but in a different department. No-No hung back a bit. I can remember she was wearing a white silk blouse with a red bow at the front and red lipstick. We had a good time that night. And that was that. Your grandma and I met, and we were married within the same month."

Muted Possibilities

Ahusband. Children. Someday. When I became epileptic, I started worrying about such things although I didn't really understand the implications of my condition. My doctor said my medication could affect pregnancy. When I was old enough and ready to have children, he could put me on a lower dosage so the possibility of a birth defect was less probable. He was under legal obligation to divulge the medication's side-effects. "If you stop taking the medication, then there's a higher risk of having seizures. Stay on the medication and the baby might be harmed, potentially." I realized I might have to bypass a future with children, having my own family. Shadyn never wanted to have children either. Her future guided by choice, not a medical condition like me. She would say, "Mom's shit out of luck." She'd laugh, a sort of spiteful chuckle.

Four years back, Shadyn secured three jobs in order to pay the bills and accumulate savings. She acted like all the women on Mother's side, preoccupied with the sum in their bank accounts, saving for those rainy days. No wonder my parents considered Shadyn to be the mature daughter, "the adult." When and how such a difference between us came about was a question not easily answered.

Shadyn was born a year and a half before me. As early as elementary school, she and I learned to answer to each other's names. People often mistook us for each other. We played along, sometimes to our advantage. We covered each other's homework assignments, absences, and sometimes even attended the other's classes. Teachers rarely noticed. In their defense, they rarely noticed anything. They ran through dated curriculum and tired lessons that were old-fashioned from the first day they taught them. Growing up, Shadyn and I were never more than a couple of centimetres taller than each other. We were both around five-foot-five with long hair and our mother's dark eyes. In high school, we shared friends and boyfriends. Until Ethan. Maybe that was when Shadyn matured.

It was in Grade 10 that Shadyn began dating that redheaded boy. We all attended the same high school and so did Ethan's other girlfriend, Melanie. Aware that she was "the mistress," Shadyn intended to end her relationship with Ethan. She never did. Shadyn and Ethan, and Ethan and Melanie kept dating for a couple more months. It took Melanie too long to discover that Ethan was cheating on her. Our high school had a student population of six hundred. Gossip circulated throughout the halls. At first, maybe Melanie heard the news but didn't believe it. Maybe Melanie was naïve. Maybe like Shadyn, Melanie was unwilling to end the relationship. When Melanie finally realized what was happening, she confronted Ethan in front of his locker at school, called him "a red-faced liar," and ended the relationship. By third period, it was all over school. Melanie had dumped Ethan, but Shadyn was going to stay with him. Students in my grade called my sister "a whore." Shadyn and I grew apart that day. I hadn't defended her in front of anyone.

For the next two years, Shadyn and Melanie avoided each other at school. After graduation, they both moved away. Shadyn heard from mutual friends that Melanie became a pharmacist in Southern Ontario. Shadyn moved to Barrie and became a nurse. Ethan followed her. They lived together, unwed, to the disappointment of our grandparents who thought the arrangement indecent. Shadyn ignored the objections. She considered herself "a modern woman" because she had agreed to live common-law with Ethan. "He should crap or get off the pot," was No-No's opinion. I stayed neutral. That was a mistake if I was to maintain any kind of meaningful relationship with my sister.

During one seemingly ordinary supper, Shadyn was confronted by the family over her co-habitation with Ethan. I sat stricken in silence. She rose abruptly, picked up her bowl of soup, and flung it against the wall. The corner of her lip raised and she laughed. Soup streaked the wall. Shadyn strutted out of the house. Soup has a resonant meaning in my family.

Serve Hot

At the boarding house, before the bar opened for the night, the family ate supper in their kitchen on the second floor, away from the boarders and billiard players. In a tight kitchen, Anichka reheated a tall pot of leftover soup on the electric stove. Her daughter Audrey chopped vegetables from the garden. She added them to the soup along with two cans of stock. "Leftovers are never to be thrown out," was Anichka's cooking philosophy. Even the oily yellowy fat floating across the soup's surface was an integral ingredient in her recipe. The pot was never empty so it never required cleaning.

Anichka's Hearty Soup Recipe

Vegetables (if summer, check the garden;
if winter, check the pantry for canned varieties).
Cans of stock (chicken or beef, whatever's in the pantry).
All parts of the chicken (guts included for flavour).

Directions:
Reheat the leftover soup until it comes to a boil.
Add new ingredients into the pot.
Cook until the newly added meat is cooked.
Note:
The texture of the vegetables may vary depending on when they were added.
Newly added vegetables may be a little hard.
Leftover vegetables may be a little mushy.
This mixture contributes to the overall flavour and dining experience.
Serves 5-20 (portion size depends on the amount of leftover soup and volume of new ingredients).
Serve hot.

Anichka and Nicholas and their children ate soup every day for lunch and supper. If soup wasn't the main course, it was always the starter. Soup was cheap to make and filled up the eight children. The family had to finish their soup before Anichka served anything else.

Anichka set the large pot on the table and Nicholas, husband and father, had the honour of ladling the soup into bowls for his family.

"Aw, soup again!" the children always complained. Anichka narrowed her eyes, staring at each of the children. Silence echoed through the apartment. Anichka lugged the pot of soup to the hungry boarders. She trusted her eldest son Wasyl to convert the pool hall into a dining room. He placed large sheets of plywood atop the two billiard tables and arranged an assortment of chairs.

"Aw, soup again!" the boarders always complained.

Anichka narrowed her eyes, staring at each of the boarders. She scolded them, "If ya don't like it, go somewhere else." After supper, the boarders helped transition the front room back into a pool hall.

"Carry the dishes to the kitchen," a boarder shouted.

"Put the chairs back against the walls," another hollered.

"Store the plywood."

A floor up, Anichka's children announced what chores they were to complete. The first to yell out, received his or her choice of chore. By then, Anichka was in the basement serving drinks. Nicholas relaxed on the living room sofa, puffing on his pipe while the children set to work.

"Clear the table," a sibling shouted.

"Wash," another hollered.

"Dry."

"I'll help."

"Put away the dishes."

"Tidy the kitchen."

"Cover up the leftover soup."

"Take out the trash."

Any leftover soup was added back into the pot for tomorrow's lunch and supper.

Later in the night when a customer passed out intoxicated in the bar, he was carried to a room and charged for it in the morning. Anichka's soup was then heralded as a cure for the gentleman's hangover. All for a price. Good for what ailed ya.

Second Helpings

It was one of No-No's rare visits. I, too, was visiting my parents at their home in the East End. Mother had made her speciality for supper, meatballs swimming in gravy.

She'd telephoned me at my apartment, offering to cook me a homemade feast. I would have skipped supper and visited my parents after mealtime, if I had known the menu featured meatballs in gravy. That strong was my disdain for meatballs n' gravy.

When I arrived, No-No sat at the kitchen table. She was devouring my helping of supper. She sopped up the leftover gravy, sweeping a piece of bread across her plate.

"Good supper, Izza." No-No complimented Mother on her cooking, an uncharacteristic gesture of affection. Often No-No would express her view on emotions saying, "The world doesn't have time for 'feelings.'"

Mother and I sat at the kitchen table with No-No. We waited to hear her reason for visiting. She had to have a reason for venturing from the West to East

End. She detested the long journey from the opposite ends of town—well, unless it was to go to a garage sale, here, in the East. It was a Wednesday. There weren't any garage sales to attend. The majority of garage sales were on Saturday mornings. No-No's reason for dropping by couldn't be that she'd gone to a garage sale and was "in the area."

No-No needed someone to listen to her rant. She had already told the news to Ollie and required a new audience, someone, anyone to listen to her complain. No-No didn't want that person to comment on her complaining, though. Open ears and shut lips, that was what she desired in her visit to the East End.

No-No tapped the plate with her long dirty fingernail. Based on that gesture, Mother knew to refill it with more meatballs n' gravy. No-No's hunger wasn't satisfied yet. Mother replaced the full plate in front of Grandmother. She nodded, her typical form of thank-you.

No-No commenced her tirade, "Have yous heard the big news? Well of course you haven't. I haven't told you yet. Let me tell you, I couldn't have been any more surprised than I was at the time. She looked awful, just horrible, half dead. I couldn't believe it. And do you know she had the nerve to come up and talk to me?" No-No bit into a meatball. Gravy dripped down her chin. She wiped the gloopy brown liquid on her sleeve. Her shirt still wore the price tag from whichever garage sale she'd purchased the garment from. The orange price sticker read, "50¢ OBO" (Or Best Offer).

Mother reached across the table and removed the sticker from No-No's shirt and handed her a napkin. She then fed into Grandmother's excitement, asking, "Who are you talking about? Who is 'she'?"

No-No leaned toward Mother. "Well," she paused. "Well, Juanita of course. I was standing in the checkout line at the grocery store, and do you know she actually stood behind me in the same line? There were how many other open lines to choose from and she picks the one I'm in. She's got some nerve. Who does Juanita think she is anyway?"

I realized No-No's question was rhetorical, but I answered it. "Juanita's your sister. Perhaps she wanted to say hello. You haven't spoken in some time."

"And for good reason."

"Which is?" I asked.

Mother rested her hand on mine. "It'll be best if you go visit your father in the basement. I think he's watching an action movie. You enjoy action movies." She attempted to smile, but her nerves prevented it. She didn't want me to see Grandmother in her angry state. Mother tried to be motherly. "Sheila, leave your grandma and I to talk."

I walked into the basement and sat beside Father on the sofa. Their voices from upstairs carried into the basement and reached our ears.

Mother said, "The Sault isn't that big of a city. You were going to meet your sister, one of these days."

"I didn't think it was going to be so soon."

"You haven't spoken in over twenty years. I don't remember the last time you saw each other."

"Hasn't been that long."

"Yes, it has. I'm sure of it."

"Doesn't matter. Doesn't give her the right to talk to me."

"Don't you think she has some right?"

"No. Do you know what she had the nerve to say to me? She pointed at the item that I was buying. It was hot-and-ready lasagna. Juanita asked, 'Is that reduced?'"

"Was it reduced in price?"

"Well of course it was reduced. I buy everything on sale. I has to be economical. Your father and I live off his small pension. And we are in a recession, aren't we? Well of course we are. So you know what I told that sister of mine? I told her that it must have been nice inheriting all that money from her mother-in-law on top of everything she'd received from our mother after she died. That's all my sister cares about, money. And power, too. I told her that. You're damn right I did. I speak my mind. I don't care who hears me. The truth is the truth. I asked her, as executor to Anichka's will, if she has given away more burial plots to our brothers and sisters. And you know what she said? She admitted to giving a plot, each, to Audrey and Brucie and no one else yet. I asked her why she gave them plots. She said it was because they had asked nicely. Like it's that easy. Like Juanita is that easygoing. I know my sister, and she ain't that nice of a person. I know what she's really like. And I don't mind telling the truth to anyone. Who does Juanita think she is? My big sister or something? Only by birth. I bought my reduced lasagna, left the store, and didn't say anything further to her. She didn't say boo back to me either. She has a lot of nerve, that one. Didn't even say anything to me when I was through the checkout line. That's so like her, on her high horse. I'd shoot that damn horse if I had the chance. Juanita is the older sister. She should act maturer."

Afterward, Mother told me she'd wrapped up the leftover meatballs n' gravy and gave it to No-No. Grandmother had taken the leftovers home for Ollie's late night supper and breakfast.

I'd stayed in the basement until No-No left. I'd watched the entire action movie with Father and then travelled to my quiet apartment.

That evening, I had more than enough excitement to entertain me until the next unexpected family get-together.

The following week, Mother stood on the welcome mat outside my apartment door. She didn't ring the doorbell. I could hear the floor squeak under her feet in the hallway. I knew she was there. Through the keyhole, I stared at her. She was crying. When she finished, Mother rang the bell.

I opened the door. "What's the matter, Mom?"

Mother peered at her tear-saturated sleeves. She hesitated and then said as confidently as she could at that moment, "What do you mean? Nothing's the matter."

"I heard you crying. I saw you through the keyhole. Mom, you were crying. What's wrong?"

She nodded. "Yes alright, I was crying. This afternoon while shopping, I happened to meet Cathy, my old friend from when I was a teenager. She dated Grubby Nails and introduced me to your father. Remember that story? I haven't seen her since my wedding, some twenty years back." Mother recounted the entire episode of meeting Cathy. "She grabbed my hand and shook it. 'How are you doing?' And hugged me. She said it had been too long since we last seen each other. She wondered why we didn't stay friends and concluded that that's how things usually go, people grow up and apart. Cathy talked. I listened. I was more concerned about how I was dressed than what she was saying. I had just gone to the store to buy a few things. I didn't change into better clothes. But of course, when you don't want to meet anyone, is when you happen upon everyone. Cathy looked great—fashionable in her designer outfit. Her fingers, decorated in diamond rings." Mother spun her plain wedding ring around her finger. It was a thin band made of white gold, no diamonds. That wedding band was the only piece of jewellery she owned. In the past, Father had offered to buy her more jewellery, a necklace perhaps. Mother didn't want any more pieces. She preferred to spend Father's wages from the Plant on more important things like the bills.

I held Mother's hand. "Mom, you don't even like jewellery. You don't like designer clothes. I'm sorry, but I don't understand what the big deal is."

"You don't understand, neither does your father."

"No, I don't."

"I'm sorry. Please explain it to me. Obviously you want to talk about it, since you showed up at my apartment."

"Can't a mother visit her daughter? Am I some unwanted guest? Do I have to make an appointment to see my own daughter?"

"No, of course not. Mom, please tell me what's bothering you. Why were you crying?"

Later I talked with Father. He said lately, Mother cried often. Age fifty-two, she'd been reflecting on her life. She missed when Shadyn and I were children, when the house brimmed with youthful energy. Only my parents lived in their home now. I had my own apartment in the city. Shadyn lived in Barrie. Mother worried about what she hadn't accomplished or even attempted in her life. She hadn't attended university or college, hadn't had a career, beside raising us children, hadn't travelled, hadn't entertained much, hadn't had many friends for that matter. Mother had been a stay-at-home mom. She had stayed at home for much of her life. Now she didn't have that role anymore either. Shadyn and I were adults. We didn't need our mother as much as when we were children.

Mother recalled all the bad things she'd done when she was younger. Our family wasn't religious; however, Father had overheard her praying to God and asking for His forgiveness. She apologized for calling Cathy's boyfriend, and now husband, "Grubby Nails." Mother apologized for arguing with No-No on so many occasions. Mother asked for forgiveness, ultimately, for not having been a "good" person. She fixated on all her mistakes, her faults, her sins. She attempted to recall and apologize for fifty-two years of what she thought were wrongs.

After I'd spoken with Father, I telephoned Shadyn. I relayed everything to her about what Father had told me and about Mother crying in the hallway outside my apartment.

Shadyn provided me with an answer. "Mom's depressed. She has been on depression pills for a few years. Sometimes she talks to me about it, perhaps because I'm a nurse. Mom has never mentioned her depression to you?"

"No, she never told me anything. Neither did you. Why didn't you tell me? Why didn't Dad? Why didn't she?"

"Sorry sis, thought you knew. It's pretty obvious, no?"

"No, it is not obvious. I couldn't figure out what the hell was wrong with Mom. I didn't know why she was crying. Shadyn, you should have told me. Someone should have told me. I'm not a mind reader. And I am damn sure not a nurse."

The telephone conversation ended.

For the next few days, I refused to speak to Shadyn or anyone in my family. They were always keeping secrets, selecting who was and was not told. Our entire family operated under a veil of secrecy. That was their way. I wished it wasn't. But it was. Mother always shared family stories. From that moment on, I had to finally see that there were some stories she wouldn't tell me.

Today, I remembered committing a theft. I was cleaning and rearranging my apartment. In my bedroom closet, I rediscovered Anichka's postcard in my diary. It was the postcard that I had taken without permission from No-No's house.

In my early teens, I'd stolen a postcard, a family heirloom, a memory, from No-No's jam-packed house. It was a postcard written by my great-great-great-aunt Olla to my great-grandmother Anichka. It was on that postcard on which Olla had handwritten Anichka's name in Ukrainian:

Анічка

The postcard had deteriorated further from when I'd stolen it. Brown spots blotted the image of the St. Mary's River. The perfume of age scented the postcard. I thought, *This is history. This postcard is my family's past.*

I thought about the extraordinary lives of the women on Mother's side of the family. Those hard women were the heads of the family, not the men. In my diary, I wrote the names of those women in cursive. I desired to write their names in Ukrainian instead of in English to reach further into the past and touch it. I could only trace the Ukrainian name of Anichka from that aged postcard.

Those women, models of womanhood to follow:

AHiYKA
No-No
Juanita
Bernie
Izza
Shadyn

I examined the list. I asked myself, *Who do I take after, truly? I may look like them in appearance, but am I really 'like' them? Am I, a hard woman? Do I want to be?*

I closed and returned my diary to its rightful place. I slipped the postcard into my purse and retrieved my car keys. I drove past Anichka's concrete pillar heading toward my grandparents' house. They weren't home. I unlocked the door. All of my grandparents' children, as well as Shadyn and I, had been given keys to their house. Each set represented who No-No trusted in the family, in her world.

I stood in their crowded living room with the postcard in hand. I shut my eyes and pictured the list of names. I placed that aged postcard back in No-No's cluttered living room, in her chaotic home, in a neighbourhood in the West End, in Sault Ste. Marie, in Northern Ontario, in Canada.

Inside, a disaster

Shadyn worked three jobs. She was a part-time clinical nursing instructor, as well as an advisor to nursing students. Her main employment was as a registered nurse on the oncology floor. Caffeine kept her awake during shift work along with the consecutive hours she endured at her part-time jobs. As a nurse, she had a "profession." She was successful and exhausted.

I was different. I became an archivist and wrote on the side. Mother called me, "a dreamer."

Since the incident with the soup and not telling me about Mother's depression, Shadyn and I had mended our ways. We'd decided to forget, no apologies required.

I knew that she had managed to get a day off from work, so I telephoned her in Barrie. Pressing the phone to my ear, I relaxed on the sofa and absent-mindedly flicked through television channels. "How's life?" I asked her.

"I'm well. Nothin' much happening here. Work, it's not bad. Life's going. I'm thinking about changing careers. I want to get away from nursing. I'm sick of all the sick people. I know that's awful to say but it's true. Sometimes it's just too much for me: those patients, some of them, so young, what they and their families go through, their stories. I can't forget any of it. I dream about working at the hospital. Walking through yellow discoloured hallways. Toxic chemo-therapy. Every day, the same, doing it over and over. Sometimes to no effect, the patients die anyway."

"Are you serious about quitting all your nursing jobs? Are you asking me for career advice? I'm not sure what to tell you."

"You never do. When you began having seizures, I supported you."

"I was thirteen and couldn't help it. Having epilepsy wasn't a choice."

"I chose my profession, is that it? What are you trying to say to me? And don't think I didn't hear from Mom that you're digging into our family history to learn more about your condition. I hope you realize that heredity can't be the leading cause of epilepsy. Other factors are involved, you see? Don't you?"

"Stop trying to sound like Mom, with the 'you see?' And yes, I realize other factors are at play when it comes to my disorder. I need to start somewhere, don't I? Maybe our family health history will answer why I'm epileptic. Maybe then I can stop taking my seizure medication. I'm sick of worrying about the side-effects: headaches, possible damage to my liver, possible birth defects. Maybe I'll visit the epilepsy clinic in London and get a whole whack of tests done. For now, I'm going to continue looking into our history, see what I can find."

"Okay, okay, I guess you're right. If looking into our family helps you, then I can't see the harm in it. Sorry for getting upset with you. I've been stressed lately, about work, my relationship with Ethan. The other day, I bought new eye shadow, to make myself feel pretty, you know? Ethan was angry with me for shopping again. He said our apartment is full of junk: beauty products, gadgets, kitchen gizmos, mismatched furniture. So what? I buy everything on sale. I save money. What about his guitars, hockey equipment, NHL memorabilia, three toolsets, two televisions, blah blah blah? Our apartment is too small. If it were larger, the apartment wouldn't look so crowded. At least my place isn't as cluttered as No-No's house. Have you seen her place recently? Been over to visit our grandparents? I remember when I was young, going into their house and being amazed at all that stuff. I can still remember, No-No had these really small Bibles, and I really wanted one. She wouldn't give me one. Grandma couldn't let go. Not even as a gift to her *own* granddaughter. I remember hating her for not sharing and hating her hoarding. I remember thinking that *our grandma* was the only one with that problem.

"I remember Dad complaining about No-No's junky house and what'll happen when she dies. She'll leave behind plenty of junk and work for her children and us grandchildren. Someone will have to clean up that mess. And the family cabin is no better. I haven't been out there in years. Does it look the same? I remember the property was so beautiful and well-maintained. Inside, the cabin was a disaster. We could barely walk to our beds because of all that stuff. Everything, so dusty and dirty. Eventually, we couldn't even sleep in the cabin. Stuff took over the space."

"Yeah, the house and cabin are pretty bad. My apartment's starting to look a bit like them, but my place is really small like yours. God, I hope that craziness doesn't run in our family. Think so? Do you think we'll be hoarders?"

"I've watched that reality show on TV about people who hoard. Every person who hoards lost something in their life, a person, career, maybe a divorce, stuff like that. Have you ever noticed how Mom stashes stuff away and then tries to cover it up? I think that's her depression coming out, oddly enough in the form of things hidden in the house. Mom misses us since we both moved out."

"But it's been years since we moved. She still can't be upset about it. Jeez, Shadyn, we have terrible genes."

"And our family, shattered. Always fighting. Feuding. We are woven together whether we like it or not. There is something in our genes. Get this, in each generation, the second male or female never lives past adolescence. Did you ever notice that? Come across it in your search? We're kind of cursed. I've named it, 'The Rule of Seconds.' Listen, first there's Great-Grandmother's second son, Alfred. You told me he died, something to do with his epilepsy.

Then there's our grandparents' second son, Russy. He was stillborn, born dead. And maybe you don't know about Mom's misfortune. Listen, I'm the first born. Then soon into the second pregnancy, Mom had a miscarriage. We could've had another sibling. Family members say the baby was supposed to be a girl. Rule of Seconds, get it? Mom never mentions the miscarriage. Our parents tried again for another child. As a result, you were born. Do you believe in patterns? In superstition? I believe in the former, not the latter. It's difficult to argue against concrete facts and sequences. There might be some infertility issues in our family too."

"I dunno, Shadyn. It could be a curse or maybe just a coincidence. I don't really believe in superstition. I guess."

"You know, there might be something else to consider. Lately, have you noticed how Ollie is showing signs of memory loss? I think it's dementia, probably Alzheimer's. As a nurse, I recognize the symptoms, even if the rest of the family is in denial. The other day, I asked Mom about it. I voiced my suspicion about him possibly having Alzheimer's. She changed the subject."

"You're kidding me? Grandpa? Alzheimer's?"

"I think he's doing his best to hide it. Last time I saw him, he confessed that he felt something was wrong. Grandpa said he didn't feel right, wasn't thinking straight. So listen, keep an eye out for any odd behaviour. Okay? And let me know if you come across anything in your digging into our family history.

Something might turn up. Maybe other relations had Alzheimer's. As a family, we have to be ready for whatever's coming."

Trapped

One day. That day, it began.

A neighbour asked No-No if she wanted to accompany her on a tour of garage sales. That day led No-No to hoard.

In her early thirties, No-No kept a reasonably clean home, made sandwiches for Ollie's lunches at the Steel Plant, cared for Allen, their first child. Allen was a year old at the time. Things were manageable. Soon, life became busier. In the years that followed, more housework accumulated, three more children, student boarders, part-time job selling beauty products door-to-door, suitors visiting her daughters. Things piled up: old sewing machines that looked like they could run after major repair, an assortment of Tiffany lamps stored about the house, vintage evening clutches, crystal figurines, some broken and needing repair, stacks of National Geographic magazines, family photos scattered randomly about, small boxes containing both costume necklaces and expensive jewellery, a small fleet of novelty boats built inside glass bottles.

No-No never commented on her collecting habit. When staring about her house, she revelled in the stuff surrounding her. Those were her treasures. She considered them to be personal and precious: cuckoo clocks (some still functional and sounding off on the hour), hand puppets, ancient and empty containers of Klik, plastic humanoid raisin figurines, old Avon products (leftovers from her part-time job selling door-to-door), bird feeders, trucker hats, boxes of insecticide, Raid for Ants, wash basins with remnants of slimy lettuce lost and forgotten after a supper weeks ago, assorted clothing in a range of sizes (men's and women's), taxidermied animals populating the house (fishing trophies, stuffed canaries, a complete grey wolf with its tongue sticking out), dry goods, preserves (jams, jellies, pickles, and the like), stacks of envelopes stuffed with unopened letters, a variety of furnishings, odd chairs, collapsible tables, sofas.

Somewhere amidst the piles were extra special treasures, such as No-No's dark blue 1940s Regal Gumball Machine. Buried elsewhere, items like a slot-machine bank, a jukebox stored in the basement, and a Remington typewriter, perhaps still in good working order. I've often wondered if she would be willing to sell (or give) me that typewriter, but No-No was reluctant to part with any of her goods. She decorated her bathroom with Mickey Mouse memorabilia. It was a peculiar feature of her house, that there wasn't a single garbage can to be seen. No-No mixed actual garbage with her treasures in piles around the house. In the master bedroom, the mattress was surrounded by storage boxes filled with unknown goods, leaning precariously, only inches away from a small avalanche of items purchased at reduced prices from garage sales around the city. The kitchen and bathroom sinks were filled with assorted paraphernalia including a complete Wedgwood Tea set, partly obscured by odd towels, Brillo scrub pads, and assorted silverware. One section of the house served as storage for hundreds of collapsed cardboard boxes stacked flat, awaiting contents and No-No's intended plan of reorganizing the rooms and the treasures found in them. The collapsed boxes had stood there for well over a decade.

No-No was a hoarder. My family would never use that word, not in front of Grandmother. We'd talk of her "antiques," "collectibles," "collection," "collector's items," "garage sale items," "period pieces," "antiquity," "our heirlooms." No-No was a "collector," "antique addict," "acquirer of things," "hobbyist," "crazy garage sale lady," "my grandmother."

Within Memories

I remember last Canada Day.

No-No called. She invited my parents and me to the family camp on Lake Superior. Since childhood, I was enthralled with the explosive spectacle of July 1st. Each year, cottagers along the shoreline would bring loud, showy fireworks that would illuminate the night sky. To me nothing was better, besides sitting next to my grandfather on our swing.

Ollie always watched the neighbours' fireworks but he never bought his own. He was a quiet man who preferred keeping to himself. No-No nicknamed him, "Nature Boy." His given name was Ollie Roy Salenko. Since his birth in 1929, he'd lived in Sault Ste. Marie, ever close to Lake Superior.

My family set out towards camp, the sedan packed with swim suits, warmer jackets for the evening, sunscreen and bug-spray, towels, hot-dogs, and watermelons. Shadyn couldn't accompany us. She was tied to her three jobs in Barrie. I relaxed in the back seat while Mother fiddled with the radio and Father focused on the road. Upon arrival, everyone made themselves comfortable. And not long after supper, No-No and my parents went to bed; they were uninterested in the fireworks, the reason for us going to camp. I joined Grandfather on the two-seater swing chair, near the shoreline. He sat passively staring at the explosions illuminating the sky and lake. A towering tree sheltered the swing we sat on. That spruce was nearly eighty-feet tall. It was the camp's centrepiece.

Grandfather purchased the lot in 1958 for one thousand dollars. The half acre property had a one-hundred-foot beach frontage. While his neighbours cleared their lots, Grandfather cut down only what trees he needed. He stripped the logs of their bark and carried the lumber on his shoulders to the locations he had marked out. In two years, he designed and built a cabin, boathouse, outhouse, and three bridges to cross the creek that ran through the property. The six-hundred-square-foot log cabin he built had a kitchen, breakfast nook, living room, two bedrooms with handmade bunk beds, and a front porch.

Grandfather reminisced, "I always liked this patio swing. It has the best view of the lake. When I was a kid, *this* was my dream. I wanted a swing like this, to stare at a lake like that, and own a piece of land like the one I'm sitting on. Don't get me wrong, I like the city but nowadays, it's too busy. I'd rather be forty minutes away from it all. In this lake, nearby actually," he smirked, "the Edmund Fitzgerald sunk. Bad storm. November gale. Went down in 1975. Some suspect there was treasure on board. Maybe one of us will fetch it one of these days. Add it to your grandma's collection." He laughed at his own joke, his emerald green eyes glistening.

Fireworks boomed in the near distance, but I focused on Grandfather's voice. I asked, "What was the Sault like back when you were young?"

"Did you know people didn't lock their doors when I was a kid? We had variety too, not like nowadays. There was something like five grocery stores within two blocks of James Street. There were no shopping malls back then. Each shop was individual. James Street alone had a grocery, hardware, drug, shoe, and women's wear store, and then some."

"When was that?"

"I'm not sure exactly. Around the late-30s to early-40s. The West End had distinct areas: the Steel Plant, Bayview area, Buckley, Steelton, James Street, Queen Street West, Gore Street."

The show of fireworks ended. Solar-powered lights charged with the previous day's sunlight now glowed in the gardens surrounding us. We continued to swing and talk.

"Way back when, dirt roads and narrow laneways ran behind shops and houses. You didn't know which were streets and which were laneways. Most roads didn't have street signs. Laneways never did."

"How did you know what to call them?"

"By what they were close to."

Nature Boy Lane, I thought.

Later that week in the library, I learned how immigrant populations had congregated to different areas in the West End, either on purpose or by instinct. Buckley and Queen Street West had been home to many Ukrainian immigrants and their families. Elsewhere, enclosed by the Steel Plant, Bayview became known as "Little Italy." Italian immigrants gravitated to the West End because of commercial areas like James Street. Many Italian immigrants hadn't learned to speak English. Italian had been their first and only language. They could conduct their daily lives without English. In neighbouring parts of the city during the 1930s, some seventeen to nineteen immigrant dialects were spoken around Steelton, Gore Street, and James Street.

Grandfather's smile lifted the wrinkles around his eyes. "In places like Bayview, Italian citizens used to shout from their balconies at people across the street."

"Shout? Why?"

"They were just talking. Bayview was like a whole other city. A city within a city. West-enders started moving eastward in the city around the 1960s. Before then, many locals didn't travel past Gore Street toward the East End. That part of the city was less developed. The West End was self-sufficient. White-collar folks considered the West End to be full of immigrants, 'foreigners.' Communities in the West End thought East-enders were 'snobs' and 'well-heeled.' They thought all the doctors, judges, and bankers lived in the East End. The boat club was their social gathering spot. It kind of defined the East. Gore Street was the dividing line between those two worlds."

A gentle rain began to fall. My parents and I travelled from camp toward the city. We had left at a good time, just ahead of the weather. Fronts always head in from the north, coming off Lake Superior, trundling past the rock-faced bluffs of Gros Cap, arriving soon after in Sault Ste. Marie. I relaxed in my apartment, drank tea, and watched rain dribble down my window. I opened a parcel from Shadyn. It was one of her medical books, and she had tabbed one of the pages. She'd written in the book's margin: "Supernatural or natural?"

As nerve cells or "neurons" become excited, an electrical signal carries from one neuron to the next, webbing throughout the brain. A seizure occurs when too many neurons, pathways of communication occur within the brain, become activated. Too much communicators can result in brain confusion, an electrical storm. The brain does not know what normal tasks to perform. During a seizure, one's behaviour, movement, or sensation can be affected or inhibited.

That description of an epileptic attack sounded almost supernatural, but I knew Shadyn couldn't conceive of anything medical as being anything but natural. She was a nurse. Her view of the world: logical, scientific, black and white. I knew her pencilled remark was meant to tease me. I laughed and thought, *What else was a sister for, but to tease you?* For me that forensic account of a seizure was too concise, too clean.

I put Shadyn's book aside. I had no use for its clean definitions.

I remembered reading a newspaper last week. I had opened to the obituary section, a habit I'd acquired from Mother, and she from No-No. I'd scanned the columns to discover that a distant relative of mine had passed away. A baby. Juanita had once shown me a colour photograph of that baby. He was from Juanita's side of the family. The black and white photo in the newspaper failed to reveal the probing green of the baby's eyes. Juanita had told me the baby had been diagnosed as an epileptic. *Like me*, I'd thought.

I sat absent-mindedly looking outside my window at the storm. I again imagined the baby, tortured by similar seizures that had also gripped my body. A baby, fragile, was more helpless, probably more frightened. The body out of control and afterwards being unable to talk, unable to confide in his parents about the pain he'd felt, endured, too young to even speak. After reading the obituary, I'd decided to never have children. I wouldn't. I couldn't watch my own child endure such an attack. I couldn't bear standing by, unable to do anything to help, helplessly watching, waiting for the seizure to end, the way my mother had to when I was younger.

Outside, the wind and dust off the streets spiralled together. The sky periodically illuminated. Rolling thunder.

Echoes

I received an anxious telephone call from No-No. "Ollie's gone. I can't find him. I called your mother. I called everyone. We don't know where he is."

"I'll be right there."

That wasn't the first time. Two months earlier, it was the same situation. Grandfather had wandered off. Second time around it would be different. It would be late October then.

By the time I arrived at my grandparent's house, No-No had already called the police. She didn't want to call them, her hatred enduring. That time, Grandmother knew something was really wrong. She needed their help.

Throughout the city, the entire family searched for Grandfather: my parents, Juanita and Murray, Bernie and Oskar, some of their kids. No-No telephoned all of them to ask for their help in finding Ollie. She stayed in the house in case news arrived. Even Shadyn and Ethan were driving from Barrie to Sault Ste. Marie. They wanted to help. Shadyn knew something was different about this time; we all did.

Regardless of the comments about "shacking up," Shadyn still regarded Grandfather as family. Because he was family.

I drove through my grandparents' neighbourhood in the West End, trying to think like Ollie. I asked myself where Grandfather might go if he wanted to get away. I decided to take the forty-minute drive north up Great Northern Road to the family cabin. I was sure he'd be there. I searched the cabin, the boathouse, the outhouse, the lot. I went up to the two-seater swing by the shoreline. It was clear. He wasn't there.

The rest of my family still searched the city. Shadyn and Ethan were still driving in from Barrie. Reluctantly, I drove back into town from the cabin. I didn't know where else to go. I couldn't stay at the family camp, close to Grandfather's constant presence, locked in memories, crying. I had to continue with the search, stay busy, distract myself from my negative thoughts.

Unbeknownst to all, Grandfather actually was sitting on the shores of Lake Superior. Not where I had imagined. He was perched on a small outcrop of rock, his feet planted in the brown sand that ran along the shoreline of Pancake Bay.

I learned about it after, that there was nothing anyone could do to bring him back. When I heard what had happened, I imagined a breeze wafting over the waves toward Grandfather's face. I heard later that he had stood up and brushed the sand off his trousers. He began walking toward the shoreline and into the waves. The sun still warmed the day. Fully clothed, he walked up to his waist and paused. The waves shifted his balance. It was then that Grandfather dove into the waves, face down, and lay there on the undulating swells.

As it happened, a family was on an outing. The father was Tommy, the Indian boy, the laneway joyrider. He was out on a picnic with his young family, last picnic for the year. Tommy and his wife were putting out the picnic fixings, while their two young children in winter jackets chased each other along the beach. Out of the corner of his eye, Tommy watched Grandfather. Tommy was curious about the old man walking toward the shoreline. He didn't recognize Ollie from that distance. When Ollie dove into the waves, Tommy acted. He ran and pulled Grandfather out of the lake. Tommy's wife telephoned the ambulance and police. After the paramedics had driven Grandfather away, the police asked Tommy and his wife to provide detailed accounts of the incident. Later the police informed my family about what had happened.

Lake Superior was the home of my family. It was where Grandfather fulfilled his dream of owning his own bit of land. It was where he had taught Shadyn and me to swim. It was where we spent every summer. It was where I visited in the wintertime to walk atop the frozen lake. It was everything.

I remember years earlier when Shadyn still lived in Sault Ste. Marie, she and I spent the day at Pancake Bay. My parents came and so did No-No and Ollie.

There was no wind that day. The water was glassy flat. Shadyn and I soaked around for a while, but we couldn't stay in the lake for too long. Even in the summer, the water felt cold. When the sun was at its highest, Grandfather decided to swim with us. He rarely swam in his elder years. He used to tell stories about how he'd swim laps from one end of Lake Superior to the other and back again. Shadyn and I were young then. We thought Grandfather was a champion.

When I heard the police report, I wondered how Grandfather could've arrived at Pancake Bay. No buses travel that far outside of the city. He must have hitched a ride. He couldn't have walked. It was too far. Especially at his age, eighty-five.

I imagined him sitting on the shoreline that day, a breeze wafting past his face. I imagined him reciting his five children's names: "Allen, Izza, Russy, Sam, Rhonda." Then he named all six of his grandchildren: "Patrick, Lesley, Shadyn, and Sheila, Dylan, and Jordan." He cycled further through his memory into the past to recount the names of his brothers and sisters, his parents, his grandparents, his great-grandparents. He could remember them all, everyone in the family. But sometimes he couldn't remember why he had left one room for another.

When I spoke to Shadyn about the incident afterwards, she wasn't surprised about what had happened. "No-No was in denial. I told you before, Grandpa admitted to me that he knew something was wrong. Dementia. It wasn't hard to see that it was

Alzheimer's. I'm pretty sure he knew. But if you even hinted about it to No-No, she'd go silent. The water gets awfully cold by October—Alzheimer's is a rougher way to go. At least Grandpa got to choose how it ended for him; he deserved that, and so much more. Don't forget to hang a purple bow on your front door. Promise you'll hang one."

"I promise."

After the search, I took a day and returned to the swing at our family camp. I was grateful that the overhead spruce blocked the sun from glinting in my eyes. I sat wondering if parts of the Edmund Fitzgerald could really be salvaged, raised to the surface. I wondered if there really was some unnamed treasure on board. I wondered if I was too close, to everything, if I should move to Barrie and live with Shadyn for a while. I wondered what would become of my family. I asked myself, *Had I become too focused on the past, and forgotten the present and those living in it? What will become of No-No and my parents, their relationship, fighting the same fight, trying to hide the same secrets?*

Breakers rolled into the shoreline. A breeze swept across my face, and I wondered if another storm was circling in. Coming.

What Had Come

Herald Hudy, diviner, water witch, messenger transcending the future, was a close family friend on my mother's side. He could reach down, penetrate the earth's secrets and those of all who lived.

Even Herald couldn't have seen what had come.

Diary Collection

Photograph of the Vovk Family

Black and white family portrait. Nicholas stands beside Anichka who is holding young Ruby. Ruby looks to be no more than one year old. Seven of the eight children are present for this photograph: Wasyl, Alfred, Juanita, Oskar, No-No, Audrey, and Ruby. Anichka and Nicholas' eighth and final child, Brucie has not been born yet. He'll come soon enough. The brothers and sisters are arranged in two rows on either side of their parents, two eldest and tallest at the back with the younger and shorter children toward the front. Girls on the left. Boys on the right. Although they are divided, all the children even their parents have similar expressions. No one is smiling.

The Vovk Family

Nicholas Vovk married to Anichka Fedorenko

Their children:

Wasyl (died at 79 in 2001; married to Mary Alston)

Alfred (died at 13 in 1937)

Juanita (86; married to Murray Showers)

Oskar (84; married to Bernie Steele)

Norma, No-No (82; married to Ollie Salenko)

Audrey (80; widow, deceased husband, Jack Daniel)

Ruby (78; married to Rick Hall)

Brucie (77; divorced from Sarah Knoll)

First Generation Salenko Family

Andriy Salenko married to Oksana Dupont

Their children:

Wallace (died at 20 in France during World War II around 1944; engaged, fiancé unknown)

Clara (91; married to Frankie Hale)

Lucille (died at 87 of natural causes in 2012; married to Paul Giver)

Ellen (died at 38 of lung cancer in 1965; single)

Ollie (85; married to No-No Vovk)

Philip (83; married to Pauline Huff)

Jimmie (died at 79 of natural causes in 2009; married to Erica Cox)

Gus (died in his 40s of some disease; bachelor)

Hazel (78; spinster)

Leroy (75; married to Lisa Pierce)

Second Generation Salenko Family

Ollie Salenko married to No-No (Norma) Vovk

Their children:
Allen (54; married to Pamela DiPaulo)
Izza (52; married to Jon Steffen)
Russy (stillborn; born in 1964)
Sam (49; bachelor)
Rhonda (46; married to Curtis Dewar)

The Steffen Family

Jon Steffen married to Izza Salenko

Their children:
Shadyn (27; boyfriend Ethan Hall)
Sheila (26; single)

No-No's Daily Specials

SUNDAY
Shake'n Bake chicken
Roast potatoes
Canned vegetables

MONDAY
Meatballs and gravy
Boiled potatoes

TUESDAY
Meatloaf

WEDNESDAY
Spaghetti
Pasta sauce mixed with
tomato soup

THURSDAY
Hash with canned vegetables

FRIDAY
Chicken
Canned vegetables

SATURDAY
Hot chicken sandwiches
and leftovers

SHOPPING LIST
- Chicken wings for 29¢/lb. at
  Dominion Supermarket
- 4 pkgs. of Shake'n Bake for
  $1 at Dominion's
- 29 lbs. of potatoes for 99¢
  at Saveway
- 5 14 oz cans of vegetables for
  95¢ at Loblaws
- Ground beef for 63¢/lb.
  at Dominion's
- 2 2lbs. pkgs. of Primo pasta
  noodles for 79¢ at A&P
- 4 19oz cans of pasta sauce
  for 99¢ at Red & White
- 2 cans of tomato soup for
  25¢ at A&P
- Chicken breast for 49¢/lb.
  at Loblaws
- Loaf of bread for 21¢
  at Dominion's

Izza's Tuesday Special

Roll ground beef into balls.

Cook and brown the meatballs in a frying pan.

Pour two cans of Campbell's Gravy (chicken, beef, or turkey) over the meatballs.

Let simmer until the gravy is warm.

Peel and cut six large potatoes into cubes.

Add water and the cubed potatoes into a pot.

Cook potatoes until they are soft.

Strain the potatoes.

Serve the potatoes and meatballs on a plate and coat in gravy.

Enjoy.

Izza's Wednesday Special

Roll ground beef into balls.

Cook and brown the meatballs in a frying pan.

Pour two cans of Campbell's Gravy (chicken, beef, or turkey) over the meatballs.

Let simmer until the gravy is warm.

Peel and cut six large potatoes into cubes.

Add water and the cubed potatoes into a pot.

Cook potatoes until they are soft.

Strain the potatoes.

Serve the potatoes and meatballs on a plate and coat in warm gravy.

Enjoy.

Shadyn and Sheila's Hearty Soup Recipe

Prep Time: 15 mins
Cook Time: 30 mins
Total Time: 45 mins

Makes: 5 quarts
Serves: 6+

Ingredients:
2.5 cups of cold water
2.5 cups of chicken broth
1.6 kg of whole skinless boneless chicken breasts
2 celery ribs, chopped
3 medium carrots, peeled and diced
5 new potatoes, peeled and chopped into cubes
1 cup of peas
1 medium onion, sliced
1 garlic clove, minced
2 bay leaves
1 tsp of sea salt
¼ tsp of pepper

Preparation:
In a tall pot, add the cold water, chicken broth, chicken breasts,
and bay leaves. Bring to a boil. Remove chicken from broth.
Shred into strips and set aside. Strain the liquid. Pour the liquid
back into the pot. Bring to a boil. Put in the vegetables and
garlic. Sprinkle in salt and pepper. Reduce heat, partially cover,
and let simmer for about 20 minutes or until the vegetables are
tender. Add chicken. Cook until the chicken is warm. Serve hot.

Family Glossary

Alcoholism: a chronic and often progressive disease that includes problems controlling your drinking, being preoccupied with alcohol, continuing to use alcohol even when it causes problems, having to drink more to get the same effect (physical dependence), or having withdrawal symptoms when you rapidly decrease or stop drinking.

Algoma Central Railway (ACR): a track in Northern Ontario that runs from Sault Ste. Marie, north 296 miles to Hearst, Ontario. The railway covers 22,000 square miles of bush.

Alzheimer's Disease: a progressive disease that destroys memory and other important mental functions. It's the most common cause of dementia—a group of brain disorders that result in the loss of intellectual and social skills. With Alzheimer's disease, brain cells degenerate and die causing a steady decline in memory and mental function.

Aura: a sensation, strange feeling, warning of a seizure. Medically speaking, an aura or warning is the first symptom of a seizure and is considered part of the seizure. Often the aura is an indescribable feeling. Other times, it's easy to recognize and may be a change in feeling, sensation, thought, or behaviour that is similar each time a seizure occurs. The aura can also occur alone and without change in awareness. It may be "a simple partial seizure" or "partial seizure."

Bootlegger: a word having roots that can be traced back to old time English smugglers who concealed bottles of liquor in their high-topped boots.

The "Business": Anichka's makeshift bar located in the dimly lit basement of her three-storey boarding house. Home to boarders, billiard players, friends of a friend, and neighbourhood folk. Such a place could have also been called "the Watering Hole," "a Blind Pig," or "a Speakeasy." The two latter terms were typically used to describe larger establishments in which bootleg alcohol was served.

Camp: a small and simple house or cabin near a body of water. What Northern Ontarians would call "camp," Southern Ontarians would call "cottage."

Cheezler: a person with an obsession for making money without much regard for the finer points of the legal system.

Chorny: derived from the East Slavic word meaning "black." May be a surname, but is also used as a racial slur.

Collectible: a collector's item.

Collector's Item: a collectible, something No-No collects.

East End: during the 30s and 40s, it would roughly have been east of Gore Street—where the "big shots lived." Today, the East End would be south of Trunk Road and east of Lake Street.

Epilepsy: a central nervous system disorder (neurological disorder) in which nerve cell activity in the brain becomes disrupted, causing seizures or periods of unusual behaviour, peculiar and often painful physical sensations and sometimes loss of consciousness.

Fire water: also called "Indian Whisky," a diluted cheap whisky typically mixed with tobacco and cayenne pepper. Has a "bite" to it.

The Good Stuff: moonshine distilled by Oksana in a pristine bathtub in her attic. Also, the liquor adulterated with inferior alcohol to dilute the substance and increase volume of supply and sold for a premium price in Anichka's illegal bar. Other names used for such a concoction: "Bathtub Gin," "Swamp Whisky," "Lightning," "Liquid Gold, "Liquid Spirits or Courage," and "Nectar of the Gods." During Prohibition, the "Good Stuff" was typically an unadulterated scotch or Canadian rye sold for a steep price.

Gore Street: in the 30s and 40s, it was the dividing line between the city's East and West End. It was one of the city's commercial areas. Nowadays the street is the location of some local businesses; however, many have closed over the years and the buildings remain empty. Crime rates are high in this area. Called "Gore" by locals, the street is considered a dangerous part of town.

Grand Mal Seizure: also more recently known as a "generalized tonic-clonic seizure," features a loss of consciousness and violent muscle contractions.

The Great Depression: during this long-lasting economic downturn from 1929 to 1939, millions in Canada were unemployed, hungry, and sometimes homeless. This decade is known as "the Dirty Thirties."

Hard: a term used to describe any female on my mother's side of the family including but not limited to: Anichka, No-No, Juanita, Bernie, Izza, Shadyn, and even myself.

Hoarding Disorder: a persistent difficulty discarding or parting with possessions because of a perceived need to save them. A person with hoarding disorder experiences distress at the thought of getting rid of items. Excessive

135

accumulation of items occurs, regardless of actual value. Hoarding often creates such cramped living conditions that homes may be filled to capacity with only narrow pathways winding through stacks of clutter. Hoarding ranges from mild to severe. In some cases, hoarding may not have much impact on one's life, while in other cases it seriously affects one's ability to function on a daily basis.

Home Sell: when homeowners sell alcohol, legally or otherwise, in their homes.

The House Special: Oksana's homemade brew. Good for a drink and for removing the yellow rings in your bathtub.

James Street: during the 30s and 40s, it was a booming commercial area in Sault Ste. Marie's West End. In more recent times, it has become a low-end neighbourhood, the location of low income rentals and housing, and the Soup Kitchen Community Centre. There has been a recent spike in crime in this neighbourhood including a violent murder in July 2014. Saultites call James Street and neighbouring areas, "James Town." The area has acquired a stigma as being "rundown," "an unsafe neighbourhood," "a place many prefer not to venture into."

Klik: a premium pink pork luncheon meat, similar to Spam.

The Lane Out Back: the laneway that used to exist behind Mother's childhood home.

Little Italy: in the 30s and 40s, it was what locals used to call the Bayview area, which neighboured the city's heavy industrial area. It was home to many Italian immigrants.

Moonshine: made in stills "by the light of the moon."

"Near" Beer: beer with a minuscule amount of alcoholic content.

Old: an adjective that describes a vintage collectible.

The Palace: a three-storey boarding house on Queen Street West. The house provided ample secret places for my great-grandmother's children to hide from their brothers and sisters, and from Anichka during times when they were supposed to be doing their chores. Only the third floor and basement were "off limits" to the children.

Petit Mal Seizure: a mild form of epilepsy, more recently termed an "absence seizure," involving brief sudden lapses of consciousness. They're more common in children than adults. Someone having an absence seizure may look like she or he is staring into space for a few seconds. This type of seizure usually doesn't lead to physical injury.

Prohibition: in Canada, Prohibition lasted nearly half a decade. At the federal level, Prohibition spanned from 1918 to 1920. Ontario was dry from 1916 to 1927. It was a period that saw the national ban on the manufacture and sale of alcohol—the time in which Anichka made some killer money.

The Quiet Zone: Anichka's not-to-be-disobeyed-or-forgotten rule to her eight children about stepping foot on the third floor of her boarding house. Her children were not to be up there unless they were cleaning the boarders' rooms. No one disobeyed her rules. No one dared to disobey Anichka (except maybe No-No).

A "Real" Antique: a vintage old collector's item or collectible.

Relief: during the Great Depression, a system of relief was set up by provincial governments to aid poor families who couldn't afford the basic necessities to sustain life. Payment was often in the form of vouchers which were distributed by the Relief Offices situated in many cities. Vouchers could be redeemed for such items as food and clothing. Statistics show that in Canada by 1933, thirty per cent of the workforce was unemployed. One out of five people was on government relief.

Rule of Seconds: a curse, prediction, proven pattern, rule of thumb, force of nature—in each generation of my family, the second male or female never lives past adolescence.

Saultite: a resident of the Northern Ontario city of Sault Ste. Marie. Pronounced "Soo-ite." In informal documents, locals either write "the Sault" or "Soo."

Seizure: a brief episode or changes in behaviours, and can include a variety of symptoms. Some people may simply stare blankly for a few seconds, while others repeatedly twitch their arms or legs.

Soup: a runny, oily, yellowy concoction served at every meal at Anichka's boarding house. This particular concoction has a long shelf life.

Stage Fright: when an elder family member dies because he or she can't cope with the stress of pressing responsibilities. Situations may vary.

Steel Plant: a large industrial area alongside the St. Mary's River. Officially named the "Algoma Steel Company Limited Incorporated," it was incorporated in May 1901. It began producing steel in 1902, when the first heat was fired. In June 2007, Algoma Steel was bought by Essar Steel Holdings Ltd., a sector of the multi-national conglomerate Essar Global. In daily speech, Saultites refer to the company as "Algoma Steel," "the Steel Plant," "the Plant," or "Essar" depending on age, gender, and current or former occupation. Working at the Steel Plant is often seen as a rite of passage. Many locals start at the Steel Plant when they are eighteen (the minimum age for a Steel Plant worker). Currently, the Steel Plant has approximately 3,400 employees. In Grandfather's time around the 1950s, the Steel Plant had approximately 10,000 to 12,000 employees.

Sugar Houses: stores selling home-brewing equipment and supplies.

Vintage: an adjective that describes an old collectible.

Well-heeled: a term used to describe a wealthy individual, someone with "deep pockets."

West End: during the 30s and 40s, it would roughly have been north of Wallace Terrace and west of Korah Road. Today, the West End would be west of Wellington Street West and Peoples Road.

Acknowledgements

This book was a family affair, from my mother going to the local public library to retrieve a book for me when I was unable to do so myself, to my grandmother telling me how "things were" in her day. Thank you for answering all my questions, as random and odd as some of them were. My words are my thanks.

Some memories, stories, conversations, and images were taken from the words of my family. I can still hear them now, the soundtrack of their voices. To those who would not call themselves storytellers: Mom and Dad, Sheena and Kyle, Grandma and Grandpa, Nina and Jeannette, George and Stan. To those who time prevented me from meeting: Eudokia and Henrietta, and Adolf. I would have loved to sit down and talk away an afternoon with you.

*   *   *

When writing *Rule of Seconds*, I sought to learn, know, and hear more. I researched the history and culture of Sault Ste. Marie, searched through history books and literature, databases, microfilm, local newspapers, dusty archives, and listened to recorded oral histories, thankfully preserved through the Oral History of Sault Ste. Marie (OHSSM). I asked questions, and questioned myself. I sat down with family members, parents, grandparents, great-aunts and uncles, and asked what it was like growing up in the Sault Ste. Marie of their time. *Rule of Seconds* is a fiction with flashes of truth.

Thanks to the anonymous woman who courageously wrote in to The Sault Daily Star back in 1938. Seventy-eight years later, your letter inspired a chapter in this book. Source: "Against Barring Women from Beverage Rooms." The Sault Daily Star, 28 March 1938, "The Women Page" sec.: 5.

I want to acknowledge Jaroslaw Lazoryk of St. Mary's Ukrainian Catholic Church in Sault Ste. Marie, for sharing his knowledge of the Ukrainian language.

*   *   *

To professors who I now call my friends, thank you for the continual support: the late Dr. Alanna Bondar, Dr. Linda Burnett, Dr. Michael DiSanto, Marty Gervais, and my graduate thesis supervisor and friend, Dr. Karl Jirgens.

This book began as my creative Master's thesis, also titled *Rule of Seconds* (2015), and completed at the University of Windsor.

Thank you to those who accepted to "have a look" at the manuscript: Authors Vanessa Shields, Madeline Sonik, and Stacey Zembrzycki.

*   *   *

And finally, this "Soo girl" has to acknowledge her home city which shaped so much of her personality - to Sault Ste. Marie, Ontario.

"Lake Superior was the home of my family." It is, and forever will be.